WHITE BUICK

WHITE BUICK

Greg Hollingshead

*For Jan and Margaret
All best wishes
Greg Hollingshead
August '92*

oolichan books
Lantzville, British Columbia, Canada
1992

Canadian Cataloguing in Publication Data
Hollingshead, Greg, 1947–
  White Buick

  ISBN 0–88982–117–8

  I. Title.
PS8565.0624W5 1992   C813'.54   C92–091339–3
PR9199.3.H64W5 1992

Publication of this book has been financially assisted by The Canada Council.

Cover photo by Taras Masciuch

Published by
Oolichan Books
P.O. Box 10
Lantzville, BC, Canada V0R 2H0

Typeset by Vancouver Desktop Publishing Centre

Printed in Canada

ACKNOWLEDGEMENTS

Writing is salvage, and some of these stories owe much to other texts. "Your God Is Finished" originates in part from a manuscript left by my father; "The Mary Dunbar Letter" from St. John Seymour's account of the 1711 Island Magee witchcraft trial in his *Irish Witchcraft and Demonology* (1913); "Secret War" from a letter to a newspaper; and "When She Was Gone" from various published materials relating to the life of a Wisconsin farmer named Ed Gein. Writing is also choices, and I particularly thank Rhonda Bailey, Don Coles, Jennifer Glossop, Dick Hebdige, Alistair MacLeod, Leon Rooke, Ellen Seligman and Ron Smith for helping me to see what some of them could be.

For financial assistance I am grateful to the Alberta Foundation for the Literary Arts.

"Under the Whip" has appeared in *Matrix*; "Watches" in *periodics*; "In the Sixties" (as "Why Don't You Love Me") in *event*; "When She Was Gone" in *Prism International*; "Unacceptable People" (in a short version) in *The Second Macmillan Anthology*; "The Mary Dunbar Letter" and "Youth and Beauty" in *Descant*; "Kingbird" (as "Dancers") in *The Fiddlehead* and (in a long version) in the *Journal of Canadian Fiction*; "The Dog in the Van," "The Comfort of Things As They Are," and "The Falling Night" (as "Into the Night") in *Canadian Fiction Magazine*; "White Buick" and "Small Death" in *The Malahat Review*; and "Secret War" in *The Malahat Review* and *The New Press Anthology #2: Best Stories*.

for Rosa

CONTENTS

UNDER THE WHIP

This is how it started. She was sitting forward on the sofa, smoking one cigarette after another, crushing them half-finished into an ashtray by her sandals. He loved her feet. She seemed to him beautiful the way an exotic fashion model is beautiful, and if she failed to be beautiful for everyone then she was beautiful only for him. He loved her accent, whatever it was. She was thin. Her fingers were stained yellow. She took intractable positions on everything. Compassionless, political positions. She was angry at ignorance and power. She hated certain governments for specific reasons. She had straight black hair that made a perfect angry oval of her face. Her laughter was full of scorn. She terrified him. He could not understand such rapid, ferocious conviction. When she crossed to the kitchen for another cup of coffee he saw that her body was perfect, and the restless force in his head that worked to turn out complete imaginary women from perfect details of real imperfect bodies went still as he watched.

She was bored. They must all go to a movie. But no one wanted to, not even him, not with the whole bunch of them, and then he wondered if the understood, obvious escort might be himself. He got down on the floor with the listings and stayed there a long time, not able to concentrate. Finally he sat up and named three movies. Various conversations came to an end.

She stubbed her cigarette.

It makes no difference, she said.

He was tempted then to pretend he wanted to see the movie that he could imagine she would want to see, but he resisted that as an old trap and chose instead one that he wanted to see. At least, with her.

"It makes no difference," she said again, lighting another cigarette. He decided that this meant resignation, boredom with the whole idea, she had not liked his choice, had had someone else in mind, had better things to do than see a stupid movie with a Canadian soft in the head from American culture.

"We'd better go," he said. Quickly she put out her cigarette and reached for her purse. Expecting disaster now, he re-checked the time, the date on the newspaper, even phoned the place. By the time he was ready to go she was standing alone in the hallway smoking a fresh cigarette and making mouths in the mirror.

On the drive he had trouble talking to her. Her intelligence, her foreignness, her political approach to everything, made him feel that his usual talk with women was no better than raillery. He noticed that he was laughing pointlessly after almost everything he said, and he hated her for having this effect on him. Why couldn't she try to put him at ease? What was so unpolitical about good manners? He fell on a chance to talk about a book he had just read, and immediately she was interested, and her questions caused him to wonder if compared to some people he thought at all when he read.

He had no idea how she would rate his choice of movie. She smoked all the way through it without reacting. On the way out he tried to be casual, embarrassed that twice he had wiped away tears. She made no comment. The next thing he knew she was getting out at her building. No hesitation, no offer to come up for coffee. As he drove home, every stupid thing that he had said to her from the moment they met circulated through his mind, and that night his dreams could have been called Scenes from a Life of Folly.

He expected to wake up wanting to see her, but his first

memories of last night depressed him. He had no sense of a possibility of being at ease with anything he could imagine himself being in her eyes. Still, she stayed on his mind. Monday he mentioned her to a woman at work, but his remark must have been too little motivated, because immediately the woman insisted that he was in love. Protesting, he blushed, and she also teased him about that. At home he thought about it, and it seemed to him that he was a shallow, untrustworthy person, and it would be a miracle if any real woman needed more than one date to see that. Meanwhile another part of him was hard at work measuring her against the few prospective others in his life, and a sad group, even as fantasies, the others seemed now. The more he thought about it the more convinced he was that he had got diverted from the main course of his life, and if he wanted to get back on track he would have to make an exceptional effort.

But this thought only depressed him more. He knew how often it had come to him. And then something much worse came to him: a memory of walking one miserable day last February into a travel office and buying a spring charter to one of the Spanish islands. Sick, he checked the calendar. It was true: in twelve days he would leave the country for three weeks. Four whole months he had spent looking forward to this trip, and suddenly the prospect of it was unbearable. Before he knew what he was doing, he was on his way to his friends' apartment—and she was there. From the hallway he glimpsed her hunched forward on the sofa as if she had been sitting there smoking since last Friday. Was it only Friday? He wondered if these friends of his were the sole people she knew in Canada, and he felt a kind of pity for her. And then he was in the room, involved in the conversation, unable, afraid, to talk to her directly, until one of his friends, yawning, asked him when he was going away. He told him; his friend replied, "Don't sound so depressed about it"; and then he was asked by her, Where. He told her which Spanish island, and she said that she had always wanted to go to the Spanish islands.

He stared at her. "Want my ticket?" he said at last, stupidly, just as someone suggested they go together. He could not believe he had heard this. Frightened, he glanced at the woman, and she was looking straight back at him, not embarrassed, not smiling. "Sure," he said quickly, laughing in case this was a very cruel joke.

She shrugged. "Why not."

"Oh Howard," someone said. "You're so easy." Everybody laughed.

Suddenly they were all talking about cheap flights, and he heard himself claiming he could get her a student's card. Much later, drunk in the kitchen, beginning to worry that she planned to use him as some kind of chaperon, he became angry when she pressed him to promise that he really would try to get her a card. The thought that she would be willing to travel with a man whose word she did not trust made him furious. He wanted to tell her to forget the whole thing, but then he seemed to catch a glimpse of how suspicious, how uncertain, her world must be. He assured her that he would do exactly what he had said he would do.

He got a student's card for her and made the arrangements. Meanwhile a friend asked him to house-sit his place in the country for a weekend, so he invited her down there. She got off the train wearing high-heeled sandals, white satin shorts, a silk scarf, and a pink cashmere sweater. It was all wrong for the country but perfect for her. They walked to an imitation English pub for lunch, a depressing place with the hats of a hundred professions nailed to the walls and ceiling. The people there, who had ignored him the day before, stared. On the walk back, halfway across a field, they stopped and he kissed her. When she pressed her body against his, her mouth tasting of wine and nicotine, it seemed to him that her passion, at least, would be as direct and immediate as his own.

"Yes," she said, though he had not asked, "I want to sleep with you."

But his passion failed to be simple. In the bedroom she undressed quickly and slipped under the covers while he hesitated in the dim light, irritated. "Get dressed," he said, frightened of ridicule. But already she was climbing out of bed, reaching for her sweater, watching him, her look—serious, inquisitive—dizzying. When she sat, fully dressed, on the edge of the bed, he undressed her slowly, kissing her legs.

A half hour later they were fighting. She had gone to the kitchen for her cigarettes. "There are apples from South Africa in the bowl on the kitchen table," she stated when she got back into bed.

"That's right," he said.

"There is no reason why you should buy South African apples."

"They were pretty cheap."

"You don't care what happens to people."

It was like a fight between two people who had been fighting for ten years. The rage she could trigger in him he found surprising and impressive. A woman he once lived with had spent much of her energy devising strategies for drawing him into fights because she found it unacceptable that he could know her as well as he did and still not be angry with her. It never worked. Finally she took him to a psychologist, who explained that her problem was guilt, while his was an inability to express anger. When Howard protested that he did not feel any anger whatsoever toward the woman, the psychologist smiled from behind a tent of fingers and said, "Now now, Howard. We're all a *teeny* bit angry, don't you think?"

He should have smiled—"Maybe a *teeny* bit, asshole—"

and left. But now this woman, this stranger, had gone directly to anger he did not even know was there, as if it was obvious, he was obvious. Unless of course she saw nothing, simply treated all her lovers with the same infuriating assurance, the same contempt for their version. Was she genuinely angry or merely contentious by habit, an unconscious master of the art of creating sexual tension in order to manipulate those around her? He decided it was too soon to tell; he would have to watch her carefully.

That night her body twitched and jolted for a long time after she had fallen asleep, and later, in the first grey light of morning, he awoke to the eerie sound of her teeth grinding together. He studied her face. What dreams went with such violence? He traced her lips with his fingertips. Her mouth opened. He put a finger inside. An itch travelled his muscles. Suddenly she twisted away from him, pulled her knees up, her breathing fast. Only very slowly did it become regular again. And a long time passed before he fell back asleep, his hand resting along her jaw.

She could not get a flight until the beginning of the second week of his holiday, so the plan was that he would take his time and find them a good place to stay. He would meet her at the docks. He knew when her flight could be expected to arrive on the mainland, and so he could figure out what boat to meet. He would find a room near the harbour.

Except that there was nothing at the docks, only a café and a few goats. So he found himself sitting on an iron seat in a hot, suspensionless bus that by an impressive series of combustion miracles crawled and coasted backfiring into one baking white village square after another. He had resolved to get off at the first seaside village, and was working hard to discount the fact that the yellowed map on the café wall had not shown any. Meanwhile he took solace in the circumstance that nobody on the bus who wore jeans—a dozen

Dutch, French, Germans—had got off yet. Finally, when the bus stopped, or stalled, in a village that seemed to promise more than any so far, all the denim began to move, and he followed. Some ducked into a café a dozen metres away. Others, hauling knapsacks, crossed the street to a hotel fronted with blue ceramic tiles and intricate iron balconies. The bus made a sudden sound like a metal cough and pulled away.

The café was exactly as hot as the street. He stood beside an espresso machine at the end of a long bar that disappeared into darkness. He ordered a beer and stood drinking while his eyes gave shape to the darkness. There was a clutter of mostly empty tables. Europeans in their twenties and thirties sat at a few of them in twos and threes, in shorts and T-shirts with American jokes on them, indolently, legs out-stretched. Everybody seemed to be just killing time. A fan with black dust like fur along its blades turned slowly overhead. Bull-fight posters in red and black peeled off the walls. Farther down the room, glass doors led to tables piled with upturned chairs in yellow sunlight. He could see a low-walled court-yard with a corrugated fiberglass roof. There was no one out there. A lizard ran along the top of the wall, froze, and flipped over to the other side. When he tried the handle the man behind the bar called out something in Spanish. When he turned, the man was making a circle with his arm and repeat-ing an unintelligible phrase. Howard sat down at a table and finished his beer. A few minutes later he realized that the man must have meant he could go around. A girl with red hair in long braids was looking at him. He smiled. She turned away. He wished he had studied more Spanish before leaving Canada.

He crossed to the hotel and asked for a double room.

No double rooms, the woman said in Spanish, shaking her head as if the request made her inexpressibly sad. He asked for a single. He would stay a week while looking for another place or until a double became available here. No single rooms, the woman said, even sadder. No rooms at all. Next week then? She shook her head. After he had made sure that she understood what he meant and was still saying No, no rooms next week, he walked away. He would rent a bicycle and ride to a less crowded place, a village closer to the sea, or he would find a beach house, where their holiday would not be confused by so many other people.

The bicycle, an ancient woman's bike, heavy, with fat tires, was a good idea. He balanced his knapsack on the handlebars and went for a tour of the island. Sand, rock, scrub. Trees stunted by wind. Snowy buildings like blank dice. A Disney sea, gleamy, manic, blue. The sun was blinding, the wind was constant and hot. He came to a bay where people swam naked and ate at a café with an American jukebox, cheap food, and beach sand spilling halfway across the floor. Most of the customers were Europeans younger than those in the village and friendlier because they were there not primarily for sex but to smoke hash and sleep on the beach. It was there that night he met a Danish girl who laughed and reached immediately for the menu when he offered to buy her a meal. Drunk on sangría, they went for a swim. Later he remembered her long legs, the surf foaming and boiling white around her pale breasts.

Alongside her on the sand rolled up in a blanket that belonged, she had said, to her roommate, he fell asleep believing that the reason they were not making love was there was plenty of time—whole days—before his girlfriend would arrive. He wondered now why he had agreed to a holiday with someone so difficult and considered how simple and perfect it would have been to come here alone and meet this wonderful Danish woman. No tension, no complications. That, surely, was what had been destined to happen when he bought his ticket back in February; the other business was a mistake that was bound to complicate and confuse what was supposed to be. Why were his earliest understandings of things so often the best? Why could he not just let things happen naturally?

The next day, back from a ten-day drug-buying trip to North Africa, the Danish girl's roommate arrived, and this person turned out not to be plain and female, as Howard had expected, but beautiful and male, the lover she had been living with in Copenhagen for three years. He could have been her twin: fine blond hair shining down his back, his pale face bowed over thin long fingers rolling giant, conical kif and tobacco cigarettes he called Eiffel Towers, passing them to his girlfriend, to a Spanish-literature student from Paris who crept like a dog into their campfire circle one night and stayed, to a wild Swiss boy who had been doing acid since he was nine, and to Howard. Disappointed, Howard consoled himself with the thought that his own woman was coming; there was no reason to be bitter; in the meantime he could enjoy this company for what it was, would adapt.

Out of deference to him, everyone in the group spoke English, though none was perfectly fluent, and so their conversations had a primary-school quality suitable for regression on a Mediterranean beach. Also suitable for the Danish boy's sense of humour. "That person is putting on his hat now," he would say carefully, or, squinting into the sunlight, taking a drag on an Eiffel Tower, "There are not so many naked people on the beach this afternoon." The days slipped by like clear, warm water. The five straggled from beach to café to shade tree to sea to village to cove to well to beach without plan and without resistance, until the sun had once again disappeared, they had once again eaten their evening meal and could wander once again down to the beach and lie in their blankets—the Danish woman had sewn together two small ones for Howard—and watch stars that were pinpricks of light in black velvet, the Milky Way misted across it—

"The stars shine with unusual brightness tonight," as the Danish boy would say—and pass around a last Eiffel Tower, talking very little, having little language, little recountable history, nothing to worry them. Howard had never lived this way, and if he were not living it now so effortlessly, he would not have believed it was possible for someone like himself. But of course it was possible only because he knew that it was not going to last, was tightly bracketed by a harder reality of his own making.

And then it was tomorrow that she would arrive. He had been here for a week and done nothing more to find them a room. He knew that she would refuse to sleep on the beach, would consider his new friends boring and immature, would despise the Danish woman and not appreciate her boyfriend's sense of humour. She would refuse to touch an Eiffel Tower. She would arrive with a suitcase full of city clothes, would get sand in her make-up kit. He saw her stumbling down the beach in high-heeled sandals.

As he rode his bicycle to meet the boat, he was actually afraid. Actually relieved when she was not on it. And then more afraid. Had another boat come earlier? He pedalled to the village. No sign of her there. He checked again at the hotel for a room and again the woman told him, No rooms. He pedalled back to the harbour to meet the later boat and on a blind curve was almost killed by a careening bus full of nuns. Where had they come from? Were boats arriving he didn't know about? Was she with those nuns? He returned to the village and again no sign of her. Cursing, dry-mouthed with heat and panic, he pedalled back towards the docks, and a few hundred yards down the road from them he came upon her in a black jumpsuit, dragging two enormous suitcases. Not at all happy to see him. Where had he been? Why did he not meet the boat? There on the side of the road they had a fight. He kept thinking how wrong she looked for this place, how completely absurd. She changed into flat-heeled shoes, and for two hours, in a hot wind, they walked to the village in angry silence with her suitcases balanced on the handlebars of his bicycle. When they got to within a half-mile of the village he confessed that he had not been able to find them a place to stay. They had another fight. A bus passed without slowing. There were figs on the trees overhanging the road, but she refused to eat.

At the café in the village she drank a Campari; he had a beer. This time it was she, not the regulars, who did the sizing up. He remembered her telling him she hated Canada for having no good cafés. At home she had spent all her time in cafés, discussing politics. He could not imagine anyone ever seriously doing that. She crossed to the hotel he had twice tried unsuccessfully and got them a room overlooking the square. When she came out to tell him, he was incredulous and angry. He carried her suitcases from the street, and the woman in the foyer smiled at him as if she had never seen him before. When they reached the room, a fine one with white walls, louvred doors onto a balcony, and a large brass bed, he told her that he had asked for a room here only a few hours ago. That amused her. She pretended not to believe him, or perhaps she simply did not and was too pleased to be angry. Exhausted and suddenly relieved, he fell onto the bed. She undressed him slowly, tied him to the bedposts with her scarves, and made love to him for two hours. When the room was dark she untied him and got up to dress. For what? he asked. She made no answer.

In the mirror as she did her eyes her face was a mask, her cheeks sucked in like a model's, her lips in a pout. "I like your face," he said.

"Which part of it do you like the most?"

"Your profile."

"You would say that. I hate my profile."

19

"And the little space between your front teeth."

He saw her eyes go dead in the mirror. She threw the hairbrush. From above him the wall showered plaster.

It was more than the figs she despised about that island. She did not like the lack of trees, the heat, the dryness, the wind, the fleshmarket society of the village. He rented her a bicycle. She was awkward on it, broke a heel, preferred sitting all day at the café to touring the island. They rode to the beach to fetch his knapsack. As he had expected, she showed no interest in his friends. Seen through her eyes, they did seem pretty spiritless and dissolute, and he could see that they were puzzled by her, perhaps a little offended by her hauteur and disappointed in him. To his annoyance they did not seem to be able to understand why he would live at the hotel, which, compared to the beach—perfectly comfortable and costing nothing—was expensive. Were they dull people then, really? Or just young. Or too interested in drugs not be be basically losers. Or were they right? He resented being made to feel that he was betraying them, suspected that they knew as well as he that he did not belong with this woman. But it was not as if he was going to be with her for life, was it? And did they think he belonged any more with them? He hardly saw them again after that. They didn't often come into the village, and he thought of them now only with irritation. Once when he saw them he avoided them. How could the Danish woman want so little, to just hang around? Who could be less like this woman of his, who wanted everything, the whole island, if only it would come to her?

A few days later, in a perverse way, the island did come to her: to steal her bicycle. She had left it on the street unlocked. They had a fight about that, and then he went out on his own bike to search for it while she put on her best clothes and sat in the café. When, at sundown, he returned, wind- and sunburnt, exhausted, and unsuccessful, she told him that she had finally met someone nice at the café, a French woman, an anthropology student at the Sorbonne, who had invited her to a boar roast at her professor's house that evening. He could come too, if he wanted. He did not want. He could think of nothing he wanted to do less than to spend the evening with a bunch of French academics . . . unless it was to stay in the hotel room alone or sit alone at the café. They had another fight about the stolen bike while dressing, and then they sat at an outside table under the corrugated fiberglass for an hour past the time the French woman was supposed to pick them up. He chided her then for taking a stranger at her word. But the French woman, whose name was Marie, did eventually arrive, in the company of a mildly distracted woman carrying a baby. With them was a small man who seemed to be in love with Marie. He kept looking at her with shy, sideways smiles as he drove them all in his Citroën to the professor's house. Marie spoke English and teased the other two on the way because, she said, they could speak English too but were afraid to try. She was dark-tanned, almost California-beautiful, but her character, Howard thought, was harsh, or was it—as he knew—that she had hated him on sight? He decided he did not care. He and his girlfriend had been drinking brandy while waiting, and a little drunk and with strangers he felt closer to her than ever before. They talked easily, slumped in the back seat.

After half an hour they arrived at an iron gate in a low pink wall that had swept in close to the road and run along it for several minutes. The small man got out to open and close the gate himself, then parked near a brightly-lit bungalow standing silent, its doors and windows wide open. "That is not where the people are!" Marie called to Howard, who had begun to wander towards it. Under a full moon that lit up a winding flagstone path as bright almost as itself, they made their way through scrub and low trees towards a circle of red firelight where a heavy man in dark glasses was tending a boar on a spit. Waving a carving knife like a machete he greeted them and motioned them on. They heard voices and soon came to a low thatched roof under which about twenty laughing, talking people were seated around a banquet table. At the head of the table was a goatlike man with frizzy grey hair. As he stood to welcome the latecomers, places were made.

The dinner was unlike any Howard had ever attended. He enjoyed it more than any he had ever attended, though it made him feel dull, even a little grim. One foolish phrase kept running through his mind: *These people sure know how to have fun.* And why, he wanted to know, didn't he? Aside from their host the professor and a couple of older men, all Sorbonne faculty members, the guests were mostly students from Paris and other young people, either neighbours or, like themselves, culled from the village. The women were, without exception, young and beautiful. The conversation—with songs—was light, rapid, witty. What Howard could understand of the banter, lyrics, and jokes was sometimes amazingly lewd, but there was no nastiness or vulgarity as he knew it. He had trouble believing that this sort of company could exist. To be intelligent and to enjoy yourself with grace and spontaneity had always seemed to him contrary destinies. He kept looking for signs that things were not as they seemed, saw none, looked harder. And then he gave up, got drunker, spoke more and more bad French, and began to be irritated by his girlfriend, who unlike him was keeping a tight hold on her reserve, as if even here she could not surrender her precious attitude of suspicion and dissatisfaction. Marie, though she sat some distance down the table, kept drawing them into things, speaking to them in English or simple French, but his girlfriend's responses seemed always only the minimum allowed by bare politeness, and it seemed to him that it served him right for being here with her: what was she but the outward and visible sign of his tight ass? And it seemed to him that there was something particularly cruel in the fact that without her and her beauty he would not be here.

Four or five hours later the dinner party dissolved. People began to wander away into the night. A woman explained that some of them would be going to the bungalow they had passed on the way in, for dancing, if they would like to stay. "Only for a little while," his girlfriend said.

In the bungalow there were bottles of liqueur everywhere, and coffee in the kitchen. There was a tape deck, and a number of women were dancing. He danced too for a while—his girlfriend refused to join him—and then he noticed that she was gone. With a bottle of Grand Marnier in one hand and a glass in the other he wandered into a garden to look for her and found, by a well, a woman he recognized from the dinner party. Except for a bit of jewelry she was now naked. When he stepped closer she smiled. He poured her some Grand Marnier, and they talked about nothing, while she laughed softly at everything he said in his bad French. They were kissing when he caught a glimpse of his girlfriend passing through another part of the garden towards the house. The woman felt him start and stepped away, whispering, "We must try again later."

Very pleased now, too pleased to be annoyed at his girlfriend, he returned to the bungalow, where she was sulking in a big wicker chair in one corner. It seemed to him that people—and he noticed that a number of the women, like the professor, were now naked—had already been trying to get her to dance, to involve her. It was so like her, he thought, to make herself the centre of attention this way. But he went to her and was very affectionate, kissing her impassive face and neck, and finally drawing her up to dance. A few minutes later they had stopped dancing to kiss, when Marie, one of the naked ones, joined them, so that three mouths were pressed together. He stepped back laughing. Marie took him away to dance. Suddenly she pulled the loose cotton shirt he was wearing over his head and free of his arms. He saw it hit the ceiling and float down to general applause. He wished that he could be as brown and beautiful as these women, and he felt a few moments of self-consciousness. And then he was standing aside, his shirt back on, sipping Grand Marnier, watching Marie dance a bit with his girlfriend, until she did the same to her: pulled off her cotton top—and exposed those beautiful breasts, to sustained applause. But his girlfriend quickly crossed to where her jersey had landed and put it back on. She returned to her chair and lit a cigarette.

For the next hour or so he danced and drank and flirted and paid as much attention to his girlfriend as he thought she would need not to want to leave, and then she was saying it: "I want to go back now." But Marie must have overheard, for immediately she insisted on taking them up to the roof to see the stars. She then led them down a half flight of stairs to a large bedroom. There she pushed them onto a bed— they did not exactly resist—her knees between their legs, kissing their necks and mouths. Again it was clear to Howard that she did not have even a sexual interest in him. But he was afraid that if he got off the bed and went downstairs no one would call him back. He watched her kissing the mouth of his girlfriend, whose eyes were closed, that same impassivity, and he raised his head and looked around the room. The small man who was in love with Marie was moving quietly along the wall, closing shutters. Howard looked at the man and at the two women, and he wondered if the man was supposed to be part of this, and what that was supposed to mean to himself. And then his girlfriend said, "Nuh," and sat up, pushing Marie aside. "I want to leave."

"Now!?" Howard cried.

"You don't want to go?"

"Right in the middle—?"

"There is nothing happening here." She saw the other man and said, "Will you take us back?"

"Jesus," Howard said.

She looked at him sharply.

The man nodded, but Marie rose to an elbow and said, "He is taking you nowhere. If you leave you walk."

Howard got off the bed. This, it seemed to him, was what he had been waiting for all night. "Okay," he said. "Let's go,"

But his girlfriend had pushed Marie onto her back, and now her hand lay spread between the French woman's breasts. "Nuh," she said, looking at her.

Already the small man was moving towards the stairs. Howard started to follow, then hesitated. Glancing back, he saw his girlfriend's thumb move hard across Marie's mouth. He looked at the small man, who beckoned sadly. He walked back to the bed. "Let me—"

"Get out," his girlfriend said, not looking away from Marie.

Marie laughed.

Downstairs the lights were still bright, but there was no one around. Howard did not know what to say to the small man. They sat in the room where the dancing had been, the small man in the chair where Howard's girlfriend had sat. After a few minutes Howard looked over and saw that the small man had curled up and was weeping, a hand cupped over his eyes. He went out to look for the woman he had met by the well, but there was no one there. The moon had set, and the stars were a million tiny pricks of light in a long mist. It did not seem to be the same sky that he had watched from the beach. He imagined himself walking out the gate and hitching a ride back to the village, but he was afraid of losing her to this place. Already he had overheard the goat-professor begging her to stay.

And then the woman from the well was putting her arms around his neck. "Did Marie get your girl?" she whispered. "Too bad. But you like to suffer, don't you, Canadian?" She put a hand over his mouth. "No. Don't simply say yes. That would be too boring. When you tell me, tell me how much."

WHITE BUICK

Again tonight Kamal was out in the street, shouting. He lives in fear that a ball or a stick will mark his precious automobile. He does not consider what folly it is to make enemies of these children. They moved their nets sullenly, aware now how dear to him it is.

At supper he talked once more of a garage.

Why did you not think of a garage when you bought the car? I asked him. Where else did you expect to park it but in the street?

* * *

Today he went to the bank and pointed to a poster illustration of a boat, a mobile home, a motorcycle, and a new roof exploding out of stacks of currency.

I need money to build a garage, he told the woman.

At the end of a short interview the woman regretted that she was unable to help him.

Let me speak to the manager, Kamal said.

You're speaking to her, the woman replied.

Only the loans manager.

Isn't that what we're talking about here? the woman said. A loan?

To me he complained, What are they worried about? I will have a job again soon enough. If I do not find work as a driver, I will find work as something else. Their fists are closed because I was not born in this country. Here they have no respect for the working man.

Nor, my husband, for the non-working man.

* * *

The sun at its zenith is low, and yet the days are warm. Gabriella, our tenant upstairs, tells me they call this Indian summer.

Let us go for a drive, I said to Kamal. To the suburbs. It will be green there.

Instead we drove towards the city centre. To make a splash. And so we did, and every head that turned caused my husband's to swell more, but I know that many were turned for me. I wore my white satin blouse and a white ribbon that is very striking against my dark hair. It was not, however, a happy excursion. So nervous was Kamal lest we have an accident that he drove too slowly, shouting at others as they cut impatiently in front of him. One day he will shout at one who understands his language, and I will be made a widow in a white Buick. When at last he wrenched the wheel for home I know it was the pain in his stomach.

Later I lay awake for him, but he stayed out polishing, long after sunset, baited by taunts from the children.

* * *

Kamal has said he feels no animosity towards his brother, but I wonder if my husband can always be trusted to know what he feels. Can it be easy for even the most self-assured of men to receive a pay cheque from his own brother, let alone after six years to be asked to find other employment? I would not be surprised if animosity, unsuspected by Kamal himself, were all too apparent to others. Indeed, that this was why his brother "let him go."

The question is, Why would Kamal want a car as grand, in its way, as the one he drove for his brother? It was not exactly a "golden handshake" he was given. Does he pretend to be equally rich and powerful? Does he want to show the world that he is a careful man who can save his money and pay cash? Would he suggest that it was sheer love for fine cars and not any kind of dependence, or vain expectation, that kept him six years in so subservient a station?

* * *

The children have taken their revenge. In the night someone has run a key or other piece of metal along the passenger door. Kamal was beside himself. The police were slow to arrive, and when he showed them what had happened, they only shook their heads and advised him to rent a garage.

All day he has been in a black mood, the fingers of his left hand pressing repeatedly at his sternum. When he is like this there is no word or look from me that can meet his approval. Even from his basement retreat his silence rises through the floor to chill my heart. In our bed he turns away, and later I awake to see him at the window, gazing down at his gleaming, violated idol.

On his instruction I have written a letter to order a new door panel from Detroit.

* * *

Gabriella, our tenant, is a curious fish. I cannot decide whether my feeling toward her is envy or dislike. She has an open, American-style manner that is very winning, until one suspects her of the kind of self-centredness that finally reveals, and gives, nothing. She is perhaps thirty-five years old and has two young children by a man who no longer lives in this city. In place of a husband she has two lovers, one for weekdays and one for Sunday evening. Her Sunday evening lover is a handsome, courtly electrician who drives a panel truck. Her weekday lover is a long-haired student with an earring, from the university; he arrives Mondays and Thursdays as the children leave for school. I see him loiter in the small park across the street, watching them go.

The sound of neighbours' passion is like the sound of their

rock and roll: a torment. One is aware of Gabriella's love-making with the electrician only at her moment of climax, but with the student the commands, cries, and entreaties begin minutes after he sets foot in her flat. (It is theatre, really; she has told me they toss a coin for domination.) It has reached the point that as soon as Kamal hears the student unlock the downstairs door he directs at me a look of such stony disapproval one would think that I was accountable for the behaviour of my entire sex, that it was not a male mounting those stairs. Kamal rises from the table and, with the dignity of a patriarch, descends to his workshop. As the door closes behind him, I quickly turn up the radio and clatter dishes into the sink while furiously insisting my thoughts are not lewdly entangled abovestairs in that melodrama of lust.

When Kamal refers to Gabriella it is as the whore. Automatically I defend her in my mind, doing my best to enter into her shoes. But when she and I meet on the stairs, and she spills her thoughts as to an intimate, I know that "my" Gabriella is only the one I am able to defend, that I am not a sister to this one.

* * *

In the afternoon, when Kamal walked out to look for work, I went down to examine with my own eyes the scratch in his car. Truly it is more a scrape, almost two feet long. I was surprised to see how deep and purposeful it is.

Perhaps it was this damage that caused me to see for the first time the beauty of the thing. The body has the liquid gloss of fresh cream, while the interior is pale tan, the colour of desert sand. The tires are whitewalled and fat. It takes one back to one's girlhood, to the colour advertisements in *Life* magazine at the American Library: automobiles like rocketships. Exceptionally well maintained, the Buick has a similar quality of belonging to another time and place. Perhaps it has nothing after all to do with Kamal's brother; perhaps he is simply nostalgic for the longing of youth.

* * *

Kamal has announced that he intends to evict Gabriella at the earliest opportunity. He will not say why, pretends surprise that I should need to ask. Indeed, I do not: he wants to charge more rent and so build a garage. Eviction will mean one less reminder of the passion he no longer feels for his wife. A garage will mean diminished chance of damage to the best part of himself.

While I can understand his ends, his means I consider loathsome, and I have said so plainly. The violence of his reaction has only confirmed my opinion. Now, like a beast hiding its shame, he has retreated to his basement den, and the pen still trembles in my hand.

* * *

How my head aches! And yet I am thinking, thinking, and today I realized that Kamal's behaviour towards the neighbourhood children pains me not only because it forces me to see him through their eyes, as a rather malevolent buffoon, but also because it confirms my suspicion that in his heart Kamal does not want to be a father. This and not (as I am too apt to assume) any accrual of disgust at my shortcomings is the true reason that his desire for me has waned. When there are no children, it is necessary for one in the marriage to be the child. But as well as helpless little creatures, children may also be tyrants, and no tyrant welcomes a rival. While I am certain Kamal perceives fatherhood as a just and appropriate facet of his destiny, I am equally certain it is one role he particularly fears.

* * *

Disaster. A balsa glider with a metal nose, thrown by Coco, the younger of Gabriella's children, has taken a chip out of the windshield of the Buick. In a rage, Kamal has served Gabriella with a notice of eviction, and she has just been as angrily to see me, vowing to seek justice in the courts. Suddenly she cried,

Look at me, damn you!

I raised my face.

What happened to you?

It's nothing—

Right. Know what? I don't think I want to live here after all.

But I do.

She looked at me.

It is none of your business, I said.

No—She folded the eviction notice, which a minute earlier she had been shaking under my nose, and tucked it into her jeans. So, she said. That's that. I go, you stay. Oh-bla-di, oh-bla-da.

You must resist, I replied. He simply wants to push the rent higher.

Tell me something I don't know. Right now it's only a third more than it ought to be. The point is, why should any woman on earth give money to this man?

My relationship with my husband, I said, is my business, just as your relationship with your lovers is your business.

Lovers? She threw back her head to laugh. Whose business is whose, again?

Please let me see what I can do, I said.

Two hours later I am still wondering: What was I thinking? That I would show this New Woman that I too understand that power can reside in more than the fists of men?

* * *

Now, under cover of twilight, following deep consultation with a patient hardware clerk on the main avenue, it has been done. Will it work? There is no telling, and I am reminded how little, despite his immaturity, I understand my husband.

* * *

This morning he left early for the unemployment office and did not notice. While he was gone I took a cloth and, after admiring my windshield handiwork, slipped inside. Although the sun shone brightly through the windows, the interior was chill from the night. The sense inside was of a moment of strictly qualified welcome, the refuge that refuses all comfort. Were it not for the eyes of neighbours, I could have removed my clothing and stretched my nakedness most defiantly against those seats of leather as gracious and cold as the hands of God.

* * *

Today, at last, during a rather disconsolate examination of his doubly assaulted automobile, he noticed. If ever they film the *Life of Kamal*, the lead role would be worthy of the Little Tramp himself . . . leaning across the windshield to blow dirt from the nick, assuring himself it was not so deep after all, when—Most sublime of double takes! *What's this!? Why*—!? Amazement! Consternation! Painstaking examination and re-examination! Elaborate not-believing-of-own-eyes! Rubbing and rubbing and looking again!

* * *

What does he think? That even so small an act of restitution could never come from one such as her?

At lunch he neither spoke nor looked at me, yet traces of energy in the muscles at his eyes betrayed his need to tell of the kindness done to his windshield.

Into the space of his silence I inserted a series of comments in an ordinary tone, the last of them,

Gabriella has told me she would like very much to continue to live here.

He did not raise his eyes from his glass.

She may, he replied, and sipped his coffee too hot, his lip twitching. I will speak to her.

Thank you, said I, and was suddenly aware how erect I sat.

In the late afternoon I took a tea tray down to the basement. It was the surprise of the intrusion that irritated him, not its meaning.

* * *

If Kamal has spoken to Gabriella, I do not know it. Neither has spoken to me.

* * *

Today I met Gabriella on the stairs and learned that Kamal has indeed kept his word. At first, when I asked if he had said any more concerning eviction, she seemed abstracted. When I put it simply, Are you staying? she nodded. Eagerly then I wanted her to beg to know how I had done it, though of course I could never tell her. When she said nothing, I nevertheless smiled a secretive smile appropriate only to such a question and in any case a foolish lie. Should I wonder that she looked at me strangely?

Suddenly she moved past me, saying, over her shoulder, with an affectation of gaiety, He's even going to fix my taps!

* * *

It is cold now, and the skies are constantly low and grey. They weigh upon the city in the same measure as the absence of my husband's heart weighs upon my own. If only I could believe he shared my misery. Last week Gabriella's rites with her student were darker even than the darkness of lust—he has not been back—and now there might have been a comfortable sense of the house grown austere and dormant for another long winter in this cold, unfriendly city. But a kind of excitement, if that is what it is, has remained with Kamal since the affair of the mended windshield, lending to his speech, glances, and movements a grave and joyful substance. In the beginning, long ago, he was so with me, but then it seemed merely a passing digression of character, for I knew there would eventually return the handsome, anxious man I preferred because it was his sad-eyed, despairing long looks that had stirred my heart the first moment I saw him.

It is remarkable how one small act of kindness from a person we have counted a foe can transform so much hostility, as at the flip of a switch. But what is to be done when the foe will tolerate nothing but kindness, indeed will on occasion lash out even at that? What act shall be sufficient then?

* * *

This morning a letter arrived regretting that General Motors is unable to supply parts for vintage automobiles. As I read Kamal the letter I braced for an angry reaction, but he only touched his hand to his sternum and went down to look again at his car.

I have just been to the window, and there he was, still squatting at the door, running his fingers lightly back and forth along the scratch, like a Christian worshipping the scar of a saint.

* * *

Kamal, who is no plumber, was busy most of yesterday installing new faucets in Gabriella's kitchen. Today he tells me her kitchen is in need of fresh paint. If she is as worried as myself that he is preparing early for the next tenant—or perhaps for justifying before the rental board a rise in her rates—then she has said nothing to me. Again today I saw her, but she is no longer disposed to stop and tell all. Could this uncharacteristic reticence be an unforeseen side effect of continuing against her better judgment to pay money to "this man"?

* * *

Tonight when I asked Kamal what he will do about the door of the Buick, he would only say, mysteriously, Something shall be done.

Could you not have it gently hammered out and painted? I asked. Is it a colour available readily?

No, he said. Not gently hammered out.

There must be collectors of vintage cars, I persisted, with parts to sell, or exchange.

You know nothing about it, he replied. Only after the event can some people see what is and is not possible.

By "some people" he means those, like me, unlike himself, who lack faith. He spoke in the manner of one who moves at ease in the realm of the miraculous.

What, I demanded to know, was he talking about?

You will see, he said and turned away.

* * *

Today, after a tenacious struggle, a dogged refusal to diverge from my goal, I glimpsed what this is about: My husband, who is not a madman but a believer in the miracle of western technology, is convinced that in a wondrous emulation of the flesh of an animal, by means of some sort of space-age fluid within the glass, the windshield of the Buick has *healed itself*.

But surely, I replied, pressing wisely (I think) on, there is no such fluid in the *door*. Surely the door is quite another matter.

Perhaps, he replied. Or perhaps it is simply a question of time. A deeper wound will take longer to heal.

Do you think, then, the door, is already "healing" too?

He nodded. The mark is not quite as deep as at first. It may take as long as a year, but it will heal. There seems to be a certain resiliency to the metal. The paint may need some touching up, but the metal, I have good expectation, will be recovered perfectly.

Here, not knowing what to say, I made an excuse and slipped away, intending to effect whatever adjustments would be necessary to fit these words into what I knew of my husband. I believed it could be done; it was an act (like his magical door's) of recovery, a retrieval of the man that certain presumptions of my own had obscured, a matter merely of several hours of careful reconstruction . . .

But I could not, finally, do it; I could manage the windshield, but not the door. There is something missing, something that I never knew, or that he has omitted to say.

* * *

Lunch over, Kamal has gone with Gabriella in her car to select new carpeting for her hallway.

It is curious how quickly a falling out of communication causes one to forget how little the other had to say.

As I watched them drive away, I marvelled how it is that amidst such grotesque and elaborate misconceptions human beings are capable of living in what they call *harmony*. How little she must understand, when even I who ponder his every movement could have been so mistaken. How easy for me not to have pressed him to know what he believes about his windshield, how easy to have continued to confuse his recent largesse-of-the-blessed with mere gratitude.

* * *

Today on the stairs Gabriella took me aside to ask me "what the hell" I had said to Kamal concerning herself.

Nothing, I replied.

Nothing, she mocked me, impatiently. Nothing. Right. So tell me this. Who fixed the goddam windshield?

Myself, I replied, less readily.

She nodded. Yeah, right. On my behalf. So he'd think I was so keen to live in his overpriced attic, so chickenshit apologetic about an accident from a five-year-old kid, I'd sneak down in the night and undo the damage? Is that it? Tell me.

No, I said. I intended that he should see it as an act of kindness.

Listen. Let's get one thing straight. Kindness like that is your style, not mine. I don't creep around on little cat feet, you know what I mean? If your husband's going to think I'm a great human being, I want a whole lot of input into the misunderstanding.

But otherwise he would have evicted you, I pointed out. At that moment I pitied her, in her narrow appropriative world, to understand so little that she should still attribute his conduct to herself. (Oh, and how she resented to see herself as a woman who would do the one thing she believed had saved her skin!)

So he'd have evicted me. That's life. My life. Not yours. Mine.

You said to do what I could.

Yeah, and I should have added, Except lie about me.

I am sorry to have misrepresented you, was all I could respond. And then, because I did not know how much of the truth to tell her, I invited her into my kitchen. There she flung herself down at the table with all the grace of a fish-wife and said,

So I want you to tell him what really happened.

And what is that?

You fixed his windshield with plastic filler.

But why? I asked, in a most ingenuous manner, although I burned to know precisely why this haste to undeceive him.

Why? she said. Because this is all your fault. This whole ball of wax. I'm just here, you know? Renting space. An innocent bystander.

To what?

I just think it's time to tell him the truth. Kamal is starting to get a little—insistent.

Insistent? I heard myself ask. It was so strange to hear her say his name. But how do you mean?

That's a straight question, How do I mean? You can't figure it out?

Not at all.

She stood up. The more reason, I'd say, to tell him the truth.

How prickly she is! An advantage of such egocentrism must be coming to know very precisely and jealously the parameters of one's self-image. Those of us whose selves are scrabbled-together makeshift functions of circumstance cannot boast such rigour.

The truth of what Kamal believes, I said, is neither what I intended nor what you think.

She sat down. So what is it?

With great difficulty—how could I bear to hear her laugh at him?—I told her about the talented fluid in the glass of the windshield. I could not bring myself to mention his hopes for the door.

When I had finished, she said, This is nuts. That's what he does down there all day? Think up this stuff?

It is not gratitude, you see, but a joy and confidence in being blessed.

Is that what it is. I still say tell him. Anybody who believes his windshield can heal itself is capable of anything.

By the same token, I replied, the holder of this mighty belief is at heart a small boy, who will not take kindly to its removal.

Oh God. Don't guilt me. He lifts a finger, you call me— hammer on the ceiling. But tell him, OK? Do us all a favour and tell the guy.

* * *

She left without satisfaction. Such belief as my husband's is not the aberration she assumes. At the merge of cultures it is more prevalent than she can ever understand. I know my husband, she does not.

Except—*insistent*. And so is the word, like a hole in a tooth, my thoughts a tongue... The curious energy and brightness of his bearing, the talk of miracles, his deference towards her, her silence towards me, and finally this uneasiness she feels ... Could it indeed be that he has not told me everything? Is it possible he believes the healing of his windshield is owing in some black-magical respect to her? Has he thought to himself, If Gabriella can heal my windshield, she can also heal my door? And has he, for this reason, become more than deferential, become importunate, become indeed *insistent*? New faucets, new paint, new carpet. Attention. Solicitude. She thinks she knows exactly what it is about, but more likely her character, her history, her habits, the crude blinkers of her egotism, have her in darkness. Not an *innocent* bystander, this one: an *ignorant*. Equally unaware that she who has loved him could never collude with her who can only most foolishly—vulgarly, erroneously—assume the true path of his enormous, teetering faith. Is this not all presumption, all mere American levelling?

Tell him? Tell my husband? At the pleasure of one who would insinuate that he has made advances to her?

* * *

40

The snow falls and falls. The great blowers jet it into the crawling trucks with their blue and yellow lights revolving. His car, under a great, dirty-mustard tarpaulin, dusted white, is parked in the back lane now that the bushes are bare, and he has taken down the back fence so as to keep an eye on it.

Today when I realized I had spent half of the morning gazing down at that tarpaulin, I carried a tray to him in his basement room, and there he was, standing on a chair at the window, sighting along the surface of the snow, also gazing out at the thing.

A moment of comedy. But laughing, I startled him. In a rage he spun round and shouted that I was never again to enter his study without knocking. Like a mechanical toy I turned and left, silenced, still carrying the tray.

What madness we have entered.

* * *

It is subtle, but there has been a change. I suspect that in her childish need to be loved *in spite of everything*, she has told him herself, that it is disappointment working to extinguish that eager gleam with which he so recently offered his services at her door. How satisfying to be reminded that vanity must err. For Kamal, the knowledge that his wondrous pearl of faith was an accretion upon a bit of grit from his wife has quite dissolved the pretty thing, and once again he is merely gloomy and irritable, emerging from his basement hermitage only for meals.

She too is in retreat, no longer visited by her handsome electrician. I do not even hear footsteps. Has she taken to her bed? Were it not for her children, running up and down, up and down, after school (as if searching for her), one would almost think our notorious third floor had disappeared into the winter sky.

41

* * *

A new development. The turning point has come, at last.
A telephone call, and its aftermath.

And another trip to the hardware store, for a ten-inch,
twenty-five-kilogram cylinder of iron with a transverse hole
into which has been wedged a stout length of hickory. I turn
it over in my hands, admiring the glassy polish of the handle,
the serious weight of the head.

* * *

The important thing is, whether he had ascribed the power
to the car itself or to Gabriella, he has not expressed his
disappointment in fresh rage against me. He recognizes that
my secretive action was motivated by a sense of fair play, of
kindness and generosity to an unfortunate woman, and this
recognition like a balm will penetrate silently to heal, slowly
but surely, at the deepest levels of the psyche. To one such as
she, what she calls my little-cat-feet behaviour has appeared
weak, deceptive, even cowardly, but she forgets that I still
have my husband of fourteen years, while hers has long since
disappeared, and her lovers leave disgusted or obtruded in a
dozen weeks. For perhaps the first six months with a man a
woman has at her disposal all the arts of timing, language,
motion, adornment, but for a lifetime with him these are not
even the essentials.

* * *

Tonight the children were throwing snowballs in the alley.
Kamal went out to stop them, lest they do terrible damage,
and was "caught in a crossfire," he told me when he stamped
in. From my point of vantage at the kitchen window, I would
say the catch was intentional.

Leave the children alone, Kamal, I said. Perhaps one day
you will have your own.

42

This was a taunt; it went unnoticed. I was only trying to move them away from the car, he replied, unwinding his scarf.

The car is protected by heavy tarpaulin, I said. They would need sledge hammers, not snowballs.

He looked at me and sighed. I suppose you are right. I worry too much when I have little to do.

So well-behaved he is.

* * *

She has been gone now five days. Industriously he prepares the flat for the first of the month at a rate nearly double hers. By the end of the year, he tells me proudly, we will have purchased a secondhand door for the Buick; by spring completed construction of a new garage.

I nod.

He touches me. I lay his hand aside.

Perhaps tonight, my dear, if I am not too tired.

It has been this way since the turning point.

The telephone call was from a prospective employer—I entered Kamal's study without knocking, and there, sitting in his own chair, in mid-argument, or mid-harangue, was Gabriella. Immediately she looked to him, and at that moment I knew her. In the same movement Kamal, who had been standing unhappily at a distance of several feet from her, his head already bowed, turned from me as if suddenly intent upon something at his workbench, saying, "She leaves on the fifteenth."

For one second then my heart was in my throat, and in that second I knew myself, for truly I did not know to which of us he spoke.

Can you understand this, my husband? Once it would have gladdened my heart to see the streamlines restored to your precious door. Now, like you, I await only Spring.

43

When construction is completed on our new garage. When demolition, contained by four walls, like blows in a marriage, will attract no attention at all.

YOUR GOD IS FINISHED

In 1925 my grandfather, working as a cemetery caretaker for twenty-five cents an hour, bought a new-built two-storey house for four thousand dollars cash.

It is Saturday morning. My father is a young child. He and my grandfather and a Mr. Cousins are standing in a large new square house with shiny floors and high ceilings. The house has a second storey comprising three bedrooms and a bathroom without fixtures or piped water. It also has a full basement with a coal furnace feeding hot air to each room. For some time, to my father's fascination, my grandfather has been peeling bills into the hand of Mr. Cousins.

In the next few weeks my grandfather will sink and brick a well twelve feet from the back-kitchen door. He will dig and cement a cistern adjacent to the house. He will install a tap in the basement for laundry and bathing.

My grandfather was a hard-working, no-nonsense man who towards his wife and children displayed no love and little compassion. My father died without once having heard his own name from the mouth of his father. My grandfather called him "Boy," and when my father was too old to be called "Boy" but was still living at home my grandfather rarely addressed or acknowledged him at all.

On the principle that a man should not fool with other people's ideas, my grandfather refused to learn how to read. It was his conviction that a man did not know a thing until he had done or experienced it for himself. To my grandfather the words *working at a desk*, unless they referred to a carpenter, had no meaning. He would not have condoned my father's writing down his memories of childhood, and he would not have understood my sifting through what my father has written for an understanding of a man I never knew.

My grandfather hated ritual in any form. He ignored all festivities and all holidays except Sundays. On Sundays he fished. He would drive or walk out and bring home a gunny-sack filled with eels and other fish from the local rivers and lakes. His particular favourite was catfish. My grandfather cleaned catfish with his bare hands, peeling them like slippery bananas.

On the Sundays my grandfather didn't fish he joined the men under a large elm across the road, for what he called a good chat, by which he meant a good story or a good argument. According to my father, my grandfather's stories were not about money or sex or the escapades of youth, they were about work. Invariably my grandfather's stories were about work.

My grandfather's work was done with a pick, a saw, a shovel. He cut ice and wood, and he dug graves and septic tanks.

My father chose to have his own casket encased in con-crete because as a child he had listened to many graphic accounts from my grandfather of the ravages upon human remains of the poor drainage found in most cemeteries.

Once when my grandfather was six years old he was standing with two or three older boys by a curve in the tracks looking up at a freight train passing when a crate came sliding off a flatcar and down the embankment where it smashed into a hundred pieces. Inside was a wheel of cheddar four feet in diameter, which a few minutes ago had been on its way to the 1901 Pan-American Exposition in Buffalo. Quickly the boys put together a travois out of willow branches and twine, but when they tried to lift the cheese onto it, a split opened across the middle, and out of the split poked the snout of a maggot the size of a small rat.

My grandfather was of medium build, lean and hard-muscled. He was physically strong. His hands were gnarled from work. The outside two fingers of his right hand had been sliced off by a ripsaw used to cut timbers in a basket factory where he had once worked. His face and neck were fissured like river mud. His eyes were hard and blue. He wore a moustache and his sparse hair rather long and flowing.

For two years before his marriage my grandfather had courted a woman in Hamilton by mail. He would send her costume jewelry, and she would send it back hand-broken.

My grandfather was personally frugal. He dressed poorly. My grandmother patched his clothes and darned his socks. She cut his hair. Under no circumstances would he give either her or his children money lest they spend it. My grandmother's money came from the boarders, of whom there were always from one to four. The money from one boarder—six, later seven, dollars per week for three meals and a bed—covered basic food purchases. More than two boarders, and my grandmother was financially independent. Pocket money for the children came invariably from her. My father remembers her late at night, making sandwiches for the boarders' lunches.

In the fall my grandfather would buy apples by the barrel—spies and russets—flour and sugar in hundred-pound sacks. He would slaughter pigs, dress them, and preserve the meat in salt. Salt pork figured so large in the family diet that my father and grandmother came to detest it. Other staples: root vegetables, fruit preserves, chili sauce, citron, raspberry vinegar for drinking.

My grandmother's life was spent in the maintenance of her home and in reading the Bible in a rocking chair in the dining room. Early in her marriage she attended the Methodist church with my grandfather, until his practice of rising during sermons to query or dispute points of doctrine became too great a strain for her sensitive nature. The church-going stopped but not her reading the Bible in a rocking chair in the dining room.

Based as they were upon other people's ideas, my grandmother's religious beliefs received only abuse from my grandfather. It was his view that when you're dead you're dead. He had no patience with what he called that live-again business.

In his teens my grandfather once travelled alone by train to Detroit, where he checked into the station hotel. In the lobby a young Hindu no more than eleven or twelve introduced himself. In a sort of purse around his neck the boy carried a picture of Shiva, the Hindu god of destruction and reproduction. When my grandfather, intending to set the boy straight, removed from his wallet a picture of Christ given to him long ago in Sunday School, the Hindu held the two pictures at arm's length, side by side, and studied them.

Next to Shiva, Christ looked wan and beat.

"Your god is finished," the boy concluded as he handed back His picture.

My grandfather could see what he meant.

A few minutes later my grandfather climbed to the fifth floor, where he had rented a room. As he placed his foot on the top step, a fist came out of the darkness and struck him in the face. My grandfather rolled down a flight of stairs, got up, straightened his suit, descended to the lobby and the street, and took the next train back to Canada.

My grandfather owned a 1923 Model T and liked to drive but was a hazard on the road. He ignored all road signs, including Stop signs, and did not believe in the brake pedal, preferring to take his foot off the gas and coast. If that was impracticable, he would pull the handbrake. Along the back wall of the garage he placed a heavy timber, which he used to bring the automobile to a full stop.

In the winter the ground filled with frost, and all digging, including the digging of graves, ceased. Those who had reached the realm of transition were stored in a vault in the cemetery grounds to await the spring of their final committal. With time on his hands before the river froze thick enough for ice to be cut, with each day shorter and darker than the last, my grandfather would enter a state of sleep approximating hibernation. But every six weeks or so he would rise from his bed and visit the grocer's on the village main street. There, in the back room, in the company of three or four of the boys, he would take a drink. It wasn't so much that my grandfather would take a drink as his manner of doing so. Unaccustomed to social drinking and having noted that the contents of the bottle were already 80 percent water, my grandfather would fill a tumbler and (because he had once had one knocked over) drink it straight down. My grandfather drunk was a sweet man of warmth and wit and a certain expansive sadness. Drunk, he would sit in the garage behind the wheel of his automobile and talk of suicide.

My grandmother, a woman who believed that a deck of playing cards is the Devil's Bible and a dance floor a Waxed Trap Door to Hell, a woman who early in her marriage had kept an ice cream parlour that failed because she refused to sell the cigarettes in demand by farmers who had learned to smoke them in the Great War, would reach deep into her soul for strength, for control of her rage, for compassion, and— reaching deeper—for forgiveness. Gently she would lead my grandfather to his bed, where she would nurse him, exactly as she often did my sickly father, back to health and life.

My grandfather did not trust doctors or dentists and never to my father's knowledge visited either. If a tooth bothered him he would work away at it with his pocketknife until it was loose enough for the pliers. When he was truly ill his care was in the hands of my grandmother, with her food and her herbs and her loyalty and her prayers.

49

As long as my father could remember, my grandfather slept in his own small room. Sometimes at night my father would hear my grandmother visit him, muffled conversation, then quiet, and she would continue on her way. It was always my father's opinion that the sexual aggressor in nature is the female, with her subtle, retiring ways.

Once, soon after my grandparents were first married and unable to afford a honeymoon because my grandfather had failed to tell my grandmother about his savings, he was offered an opportunity by the village mortician to deliver a hearse to Valleyfield, Quebec, and to return behind the wheel of another. On the way, my grandparents came upon an Indian woman lying by the roadside, apparently wounded or ill. My grandmother insisted they pick her up, and so my grandfather made room in the back. Thirty minutes later they stopped for water, but the woman was already dead. At Grafton, Wicklow, Colborne, nobody wanted her, so my grandfather dug a grave with his hands on a Lake Ontario beach and buried her, marking the spot with a pile of stones. Outside Valleyfield, a car full of teenagers passed the hearse and shouted, "Hey old man! Your truck's on fire!" My grandmother, a nervous passenger, threw herself out the door and broke her collarbone.

Every once in a while the dynamics within my grandparents' household were brought into heightened focus by the arrival, in a vested suit, on a shiny bicycle with an oversized sprocket, of Uncle Cy. The arrival of Uncle Cy could be compared to the descent of an angel from heaven, or at least to a visit by the Prime Minister. Uncle Cy was a citizen of this world and an expert on the next. He was a man of immense charm, a consummate gentleman. Among the neighbours Uncle Cy inspired an attitude close to reverence. For my grandmother amidst her fourteen-hour day of domestic labour, the presence of Uncle Cy in my grandfather's house must have seemed a blessing.

Uncle Cy's pure white hair and white goatee, his pink face and soft hands, belied the fact that the man was a survival machine. The life lived by Uncle Cy, the life of a professional freeloader, required the skill of a rope walker and the guts of a burglar. Gradually over the months, for my grandfather the honour of Uncle Cy's presence would lose its lustre. For one thing, in Uncle Cy my grandmother and her conventional yet preposterous religious views concerning the torments of hellfire for the wicked and an eternity at the harp for the virtuous, found an ally and a seconder. My grandfather did enjoy a good chat, and the heat and frequency of religious disputation in the house increased with the participation of Uncle Cy. But the obvious unresolvability of these issues by the living must itself have come to oppress my grandfather in his commitment to the material world. For another thing, Uncle Cy, having lost a large investment in Stanley Steamer shares, harboured a terrible bitterness toward the coming automobile and vowed more than once that society would rue the day it fell in love with the monstrous gasoline buggy. My grandfather was of the contrary opinion. But probably the main reason Uncle Cy's presence would eventually pall for my grandfather was that though Uncle Cy carried on a gold chain that looped across his vest a large gold pocketwatch with the family name printed across the face and was consequently rumoured to have worked in a family watchworks somewhere, Uncle Cy was not positively known to have worked a day in his life, and if he did work, it was certainly not while under the roof of my grandfather, slogging ten or eleven hours a day at the end of a pick or shovel to feed and pamper this goateed sponge.

But my grandfather was nothing if not an indirect man, and Uncle Cy was nothing if not a student of human behaviour, and before any embarrassing crisis, any *being asked*, Uncle Cy would make his announcement, strap his few belongings (among them, my father happened to know, a derringer in a malachite case) to his bicycle, fasten his pantclip, wave, and push off. There would be tears in my grandmother's eyes and relief on my grandfather's face as they turned back once more to their narrow, difficult lives. But time would pass, a year would come around, and another, and one day our relative would cycle into view, to be received with fervour and gratitude.

My father shared my grandfather's faith in certain features of the modern world. To my father antiquity meant, simply, dirt. He believed in asphalt and development and the commotion of progress. He believed in the eventual, infinite adaptability of the human animal. If life could crawl out of the sea and grow lungs it could adjust to anything. The house my grandfather bought in 1925 was situated at the top of a hill near a road that over the years became a busy highway. Normally my grandfather refused to leave home without a destination of his own choosing, but one year my uncle rented a cottage, in the north, which he convinced my grandparents to take for a week. By noon of the second day they were back at home. The silence had made it impossible for my grandfather to sleep. He missed the constant sound of cars and big trucks gearing down for the grade.

It seems to me that aside from certain anecdotes, our family has bracketed my grandfather in a silence larger than his own. His origins are as mysterious to me as Uncle Cy's. My father's story begins with his own first memories, his mother's ice cream parlour, the wrought-iron chairs with wooden seats and the wrought-iron tables, a glass case that bubbled out, filled with candy, a world of wonder. His father was already twenty-six. When I was a child I did not know how to formulate the questions. When I was older my parents and my father's brother would tell me, "Ask your aunt," because Aunt Ada, my father's sister, had made herself an expert in local history. But Ada would never tell me anything except what buildings in the town were built when, and now she is dead. The cause of the silence seems more likely to be shame than lack of interest. These are not dull people. But whether the shame arises from the fact that my grandfather was a digger of graves and septic tanks, or whether it arises from an illegitimacy somewhere, or from his failure to show love for his family, or from some other cause, some particular act or acts of hard-heartedness that I have never been told about, or from a combination of these and perhaps other things, I will never know.

My father's last three years of schooling, Grades Six, Seven, and Eight, were spent in a four-room schoolhouse under the eye of a Mr. Marsh, who carried a strap in his hip pocket, squirted tobacco juice at the mice, and sometimes went two or three days at a time without speaking. My father lists the subjects taught by Mr. Marsh as Obedience, Discipline, Math, History, Geography, Latin, Algebra, and Trigonometry, in that order. Once Mr. Marsh threw a schoolbag at a student so hard that when the student ducked it shattered a blackboard. My father was regularly slapped, strapped, and beaten by Mr. Marsh. One day when Mr. Marsh took a swing at my father, my father pulled back his head, and Mr. Marsh smashed his hand into the wall. My father was expelled. But first Mr. Marsh picked him up by the back of the neck and the seat of the pants and threw him down the nearest flight of stairs. My father went home expecting the same again from his father, who to his amazement instead spoke to a trustee and eventually to the principal, and my father was allowed to return to school. "All was forgiven," he writes. "No recrimination. No vindictiveness. Marsh was a wonderful man and schoolmaster."

In the later years of my childhood, in what seemed a different age from the one when my grandfather had been alive, I would see, moving through the village, my grandfather's last partner in the septic tank business. This cadaverous figure was a giant. He stood six feet ten inches, and he walked with that peculiar stiff gait of wolfhounds who are too big to be dogs and have taken on the movements of horses. His face was set in a toothless sanguine mask, and his eyes had the shyness and fear of a dog's that has spent its life as an object of astonishment and dismay. When I was little I saw all this, with a different understanding. Watching this man walk down the street I was proud in the knowledge that I should have a connection to such an appropriately exotic creature from the days of my grandfather.

In childhood my father was not physically weak, but he was susceptible to every spring epidemic: measles, chicken pox, croup, scarlet fever. When he was very young, the practice was to quarantine the household—a poster nailed by the Health Department to the front door—but as he grew older the fashion changed. To avoid restricting entire families, the health authorities placed children with various communicable diseases in single houses, something like short-term group homes. It was in houses like these that my father also contracted mumps, scabies, and rheumatic fever.

When, after a decorous four-year courtship, my Uncle Devon, a respectable twenty-four-year-old farmer, considered within the community an excellent catch, proposed to my Aunt Ada, who was twenty-one, Ada said yes, so Devon spoke to my grandfather who said, "This is very sudden," but did, ungraciously, in time, give his assent. On June 6, 1931, my father, aged twelve, escaped from the quarantine home where he would soon contract St. Vitus Dance to the front porch of his parents' house to watch the wedding through the window. When he saw that his brother, aged nineteen, was giving away the bride, he understood that his father had not come and knew immediately that he had gone fishing. Six and subsequently thirteen years later, my grandfather also fished during the weddings of his two sons. Twenty-two years later, I stood on my Aunt Ada's front porch looking in through the window to watch my grandfather's funeral. Later, against my will, I was taken inside to "pay my respects" to the contents of the shining mahogany box on the piano bench, and I could see right away that the old man had not come to this ceremony either.

After the departure of my father's older brother for a wild life of motorcars and women in the city, and of his sister Ada for marriage and life on the farm, my father lived alone with his parents and the boarders. Since my grandfather rarely acknowledged him and was generally hostile, my father had great difficulty understanding—accepting, more likely—what was expected of him. One night when my father was sixteen he happened to come in earlier than usual to find my grandfather waiting up to ask where he had been and what he had been doing. Since my father was feeling virtuous—he was early!—and since what he'd been doing was hanging around the gas station, hitching rides on trucks, smoking cigarettes, playing poker for money, and fooling around with girls, he was reluctant to say, and since my grandfather (rightly, as my father knew) believed that anyone out after eleven is up to no good, the questions quickly led to shouting. When my father angrily left the kitchen through the swing door, headed for bed, my grandfather, who had never laid a hand on him, followed, in his sock feet, into the hall, and there did just that: laid a hand on my father's arm, to stop him from climbing the stairs. My father threw off that hand so violently that my grandfather fell down, hard, on the shiny floor. That night my father packed a few things without knowing what they were and left home for good.

My father died eight years ago in a suburban hospital, of pneumonia after a stroke suffered one afternoon at the racetrack, where he used to go, alone, when he could make the time. Each morning for seven days of still heat and blue sky, my mother and I drove to the hospital to watch him in his deepening sleep. Every so often one of us would go and talk a couple of nurses into vacuuming his lungs. One morning as we crossed the lot towards the hospital building, my mother mentioned that my grandfather had died the same way, over several days, after a stroke. But she and my father had visited him only once or twice, and then for only a few minutes.

"We were young in those days," she said. "Much more interested in parties."

Not long after both my grandparents died, my Aunt Ada and Uncle Devon were cleaning out the old house in preparation for selling it when they found, in the attic, all the gifts that my grandfather had been given since he had moved his family into that house. The gifts were unopened. I heard about this later, years later, and I thought of how unhappy a gift could make my father. Grey-faced and bloodshot on Christmas morning, he would hold in his hands some tie or dressing gown, however elegant or expensive, and gaze at it with a kind of queasy distaste. He would thank the giver with a false smile, despair in his eyes, and then he would set the gift aside, out of sight, and never pick it up willingly again.

I have one memory of my grandfather alive. I am looking up at him as he works, hatless, wondrously tall, in his garden. His clothes are an old man's clothes. The sun is high in the sky behind him. He has an old man's moustache, an old man's fleshless face and watery eyes. His hand on the shovel is deformed, and when it moves across his mouth with a handkerchief it shakes.

THE DOG IN THE VAN

It was an old blue Chevy van with newly painted white bumpers. Towards the rear of each side panel was a small plastic window in the shape of a teardrop. The van must have arrived in the parking lot each weekday morning at some time before eight-thirty because that was when the Crossleys arrived, and it was always there first. On days the Crossleys left as late as five-thirty or six it was still there; and if it were not in a different spot when they arrived the next morning they might have supposed it never moved at all.

Both windows were rolled up tight and the dog usually sat at one of them watching the Crossleys leave their car and walk the parking lot to the Arts Building. If Jan Crossley detoured to approach the van, the animal would neither bark nor look at her in the beseeching, tail-thumping way of some dogs but would pretend that anything else was more interesting: the next car arriving, a styrofoam coffee cup rolling around on the pavement, a fly dying in the dust of the dashboard.

Seeing the dog turn away from his wife, Dick Crossley thought how perfectly Kipling expresses Mowgli's humanity by his ability to stare down every animal in the jungle, but Jan cried, "Aw, he's self-conscious!"

"Come on, Jan."

"Look! He's just a baby!"

Dick took a step closer to study the animal through the muddy window. "An adolescent, actually," he said. "A mongrel. With a lot of German Shepherd in him."

"He's beautiful!"

Dick sighed and glanced up at the Arts Building. He

imagined a half dozen of their colleagues watching from office windows.

"Oh Dick. I just wish we lived in the country."

Dick was looking at his watch. "Listen. I've got exactly fifteen minutes to get that Kipling lecture together."

"Dick! He's been shot!"

There was a long wound on the dog's left foreleg that looked like a graze from a .22. As they stared at the wound the dog gave its foreleg a lick and lifted pathetic eyes.

"He knew we were talking about his leg," Jan said as Dick walked her towards the Arts Building.

"Uh huh."

Usually the dog sat in the front seat of the van and was therefore visible from a distance, often before the Crossleys got out of their car. The first time Jan noticed that the dog was sitting in the driver's seat, she cried, "Look, Dick! He wants to drive away!" To which Dick replied that obviously the dog sat in whatever seat the sun shone on. When the dog was not visible he was sleeping, usually on one of the seats, paws dangling, or in the space between the seats. Occasionally, not often, he slept in the back of the van, which was more or less empty. If the dog slept in the back, Jan was able to see him only by making a visor with her hands and putting her face right up to the rear window. When she did this, Dick became anxious and walked on ahead. He was afraid that a colleague would see her or that she would startle the dog into sudden noise. He thought of dogs going wild with savage barking in the backs of parked station wagons. But nothing like that ever happened with this dog. As Jan reported to Dick, if the dog saw her he would open his eyes and close them without even lifting his head, or he would lift his head and look away as if scrutinizing the dark inner wall of the van.

One evening Jan said that Dan Cavanaugh had told her

sometimes he heard howling from the van on his way to his eight o'clock class. "Dan gets here at seven in the morning," Jan said. "Which means that poor dog is locked up inside that van for eleven hours a day at the very least."

"He probably gets walked," said Dick, who was reading the paper.

"I'd be very surprised."

Dick looked up in mild amusement. "Why?"

"Because somebody who would lock a dog in a van for eleven hours a day is not likely to care if the dog goes for a walk or not."

Dick did not long consider the logic of this before he returned to the paper. "He would if the dog shat in the van."

Jan drank her coffee and gazed out at the night. "How could I find out."

"Chalk the dog's feet," Dick said, not looking up.

"Very funny."

For a long time then Dick was aware of Jan staring at the top of his head, where the hair was thinning. Finally she said, "I'll chalk the handles!"

"Oh fine. Not in broad daylight, please."

"Nobody'll notice."

The next morning Jan took a piece of chalk from one of the classrooms and went out into the parking lot and chalked the handles. That evening on their way to the car she checked and reported that they had not been touched.

"Did you do the back door?" Dick asked as they pulled out of the parking lot.

"Damn," Jan said quietly. "Tomorrow."

Complete chalking confirmed that the next day, anyway, the dog had been given no walk. That evening Jan got into the car angry. "I'm reporting this," she said. "It's not fair."

"Jan, people have been doing this kind of thing to animals

59

for thousands of years. What's the difference between tying a dog to a stake all day and leaving it in a van?"

"That's like saying what's wrong with concentration camps when genocide happens all the time."

"It is not."

"He's got no air! He can't even walk in a proper circle! He can't go to the bathroom!"

"I'd be surprised if a dog of mine went to my bathroom!" Dick laughed, but his eyes were on Jan and they were anxious.

Jan stared out the window. "I want to complain to somebody."

"You've been complaining to me for six weeks. Is there something I'm supposed to be doing that I'm not?"

Jan looked at him, faintly startled. "What's it got to do with you?"

"Or you. I mean, aren't you getting a little obsessive about this? So somebody leaves his dog in his van. It's his dog, it's his van. The dog seems happy. The owner's probably happy. Term's almost over, so I'm happy. Why can't you be?"

"I told you. I think it's cruel."

"Call the S.P.C.A."

Jan did and was told that they would take the dog away only if it was visibly maltreated or sick.

When she complained to Dick about this response, he said, "Right. How about a petition on the windshield."

Jan considered this, her eyes studying his face, which he kept impassive. "A note," she finally said.

"Saying what."

"That I think it's inhuman."

"Inhumane?"

"Both."

"Are you sure a German Shepherd owner who drives a beat-up 1971 van with a Playboy bunny rabbit hanging from the rearview is going to even recognize what you are saying?

It would probably do as much good as reading the note to the dog."

"Maybe there's a university law about pets on campus."

"Careful. The Dean's secretary brings her cat to the office. You wouldn't want to cross the Dean's secretary."

"Dick, why can't you see this?"

"I've said already, in a whole lot of different ways, why I can't see this. Jan, you're obsessed."

"Now it's my problem."

"I'm not saying the dog is not being maltreated— though I have to admit I can't see it from the animal's appearance or behaviour. I am saying that you do have this way of focussing on things and not letting them go. You're like a dog yourself, the way you're always worrying some bone—"

"Now I'm the dog."

"Jan, be reasonable."

The next day Jan called Campus Security, but they had no interest in the dog as long as it stayed in the van. They asked if the parking sticker on the windshield was valid until the end of term. Jan went out and checked and called them back to say that it was. In that case, Campus Security said, it was no concern of theirs.

For some time Jan had been losing sleep over the dog in the van, though usually by the end of second term she had trouble sleeping anyway. She began to talk about the owner of the van, who it might be. Like Dick's, her office over-looked the parking lot. One evening she stayed on to wait for the owner to leave for the day. She kept an eye on the lot until midnight, when she fell asleep at her desk. By two a.m. the van was gone.

"It must be a student," she told Dick as she got into bed at a quarter to three, "studying for exams. Some thoughtless kid. You know what this means, don't you."

"What—" said Dick, who was not awake.

"Today that poor dog was in that van for at least seventeen hours."

Their colleagues had started making little jokes to Dick about Jan's obsession. She talked to everybody. Dick wanted the term to end so she could relax in the sun and the long evenings of summer and recover from the fatigue that had to be what caused her to narrow down like this.

"Maybe I should just confront him," Jan said one day. "Maybe he's even one of my students. Maybe I should offer to take his dog for a walk. You know what some of their schedules are like. And this term I've got that two hour break—"

"Don't confront the owner," Dick said wearily. "Don't offer to walk his dog for him. Support the S.P.C.A., leave a note of outrage on the windshield, get up a petition, buy a handgun and shoot the dog, but do not confront the owner."

"Why are you being so impatient with me?"

"Because it's all I ever hear from you— Jan? Here's an idea. We'll get another dog. A small one like Fergie. How would that be?"

Two years previous they had bought a Lakeland terrier, but one Sunday morning it was hit by a car. Dick could still see Jan bawling up the driveway in her nightgown holding the smashed little thing in her outstretched hands. It was like something out of Greek tragedy.

"No," she now said carefully. "I think we should live in the country before we get another dog."

"Right. It's a sign. We'll move to the country. We've talked about this for three years. We'll move to the country and buy a proper dog. A big dog. We'll teach evenings, three days a week, avoid rush hours—"

"Dick? Moving to the country is not the point here."

"What is the point."

"I'm worried about the dog."

One warm morning in April, in the last week of lectures, they arrived to find one of the van's windows open and the dog asleep in the sun on the pavement by the front wheel. They parked nearby, and the sound of their slamming doors had the dog on its feet, ready to bolt. They approached cautiously, because its face as it stood sniffing the air told nothing of what it would do. But it was still sniffing the back of Jan's hand as she placed the other on its neck then scratched and rubbed behind its ears. When Jan stood up she held her fingers under Dick's nose. They smelled of dog. Dick drew back. The dog was stretching, its back legs straight out behind, its mouth in a grimace, and in that position, at the very height of its stretch, it fell over.

"He's sick!" Jan cried, kneeling beside the dog.

"Don't touch it! Get back!"

The dog's eyes opened. It looked at Jan and Dick a moment then straight ahead, as if concentrating. Its paws twitched once, twice. One eye seemed to swell. It made no attempt to move.

Dick had pulled Jan to her feet, and now they stood, his hands at her shoulders, staring down at the dog. Their briefcases lay on the pavement behind them. A cool breeze came across the pavement. It flattened a section of the animal's fur.

Suddenly the dog scrambled to its feet, panting. With its tail going, its muzzle crinkled, its lips lifted off its yellow teeth, it came slowly, possibly unsteadily, towards Jan. Dick pulled her back, muttering, "Let's get out of here."

Jan let herself be walked away. The dog stood watching them go. Twice it barked, tail going, as if it thought they were playing, and then it circled to lie down again in the sun.

"He was smiling," Jan said as Dick hurried her into the building. "Have you ever seen a dog smile before?"

"Dogs don't smile."

"Maybe falling over is a trick he can do—"

"Like drawing blood," Dick said. "I'm calling the S.P.C.A. You don't take chances with rabies. It lives in the country. Sometimes there's mud on the tires. It's probably been bitten by a fox, or a skunk."

Dick phoned the S.P.C.A., and when the Crossleys left that afternoon at 3:30, the dog was gone. Jan insisted they leave a note on the windshield explaining what had happened.

"OK. Just don't sign it or give our number."

That was Thursday. The weekend was Easter. On Saturday Jan called the S.P.C.A., but they had no record of the dog. She was told that if she wanted to claim it she would have to come and identify it. "What if they've already put him down and he wasn't sick?" she asked Dick.

Dick took her hand. "Jan, it's Easter Sunday, and tomorrow's Easter Monday. Why don't we relax. We won't think about the dog. Wherever it is at this moment, it almost certainly is not in the van. And they don't put down healthy dogs who haven't bitten anybody." At least, Dick did not think so.

On Tuesday they did not have to be at the university until ten-thirty. When they arrived the dog was back in the van.

"I'm so relieved!" Jan cried. This time when she approached, the dog barked happily. In shock Dick saw her hand go to the door handle and the door open. The dog jumped down past her and came wagging over to him, sniffing at his crotch. Dick stepped back.

"Come on, boy," Dick said. "Back in the van—"

"Oh, Dick. Please. Let's let him walk around a bit."

Dick left Jan in the parking lot rubbing the dog's neck. He imagined rushing her to the hospital for stitches and shots.

When they left at three, the dog was asleep on the pavement by the driver's side. "There. See?" Dick said. "The owner's been by."

"I left a note," Jan explained quickly as she went over to give the dog a scratch. "I said we wouldn't call anybody if he could just not be locked up in the van all the time."

Dick rolled his eyes and walked on.

On a dim afternoon later that week Dick was on his way to the library to return books. He was in a hurry because it was going to rain. As he passed the Java Joint he noticed Jan sitting with a young guy in a denim jacket. She saw Dick through the window and waved.

"Dick, this is Larry. It's his dog."

Larry had worked hard to develop his upper body, which he carried like something blown in glass. His fine blond hair had been done by a hairdresser. He wore a gold necklace, a ring with an amethyst in it, and a massive I.D. bracelet. He had pale blue eyes, a squarish, handsome face, and a little tick of a sunburned nose.

"Hello, Larry," Dick said as they shook hands. "Jan's been worried about that dog of yours."

"She told me," Larry said. "I just hate like heck to leave Mr. D alone all day, but you guys should see my timetable, eh?"

"Larry's in Business," Jan said. Her eyes were anxious.

Dick did not like the look of Larry. "When it fell over," he told him, "we thought it had rabies. I hope you didn't mind—"

"Oh, no problem. I just swung down on Saturday and picked him up. He was one freaked-out pup."

"What was it?"

"What."

"Why did your dog fall over?"

Larry shrugged. "Like I was telling your wife. Hey,

there's nothing Mr. D likes better than a super-good scratch."

"D for dog," Jan explained.

"No, Larry," Dick said. "It fell over."

Larry shook his head. He sure did not know anything about that.

"Maybe its leg gave out," Dick suggested irritably. "It was shot, wasn't it?"

"Aw yeah," Larry replied. "That was just a graze, eh. He's sure a-scared of loud noises now though."

"What did the S.P.C.A. say?"

"Oh, they said he's fine. Really good."

When Dick noticed that he was standing talking to this mendacious fool with an armful of heavy books, he excused himself and ducked out, hunching to protect the books as if the rain had already started. It was so like Jan to try to handle everything on her crackbrained idea of a human level. Never mind the time and emotion she wasted, or that it was none of her business, or that Larry was nobody to have coffee with.

Dick barely had time to get back to the Arts Building before the storm hit. High in his office he stood and watched the rain come down and the lightning glare white and flicker for long seconds. There were great cracks of thunder like rock splitting, rumbling declensions of sound that shook the air. Suddenly a flash of brown at the passenger window of the van caught Dick's eye, and when he looked he saw the dog's face smash against the window and disappear, smash against the window and disappear.

After hesitating, Dick carefully unfolded the plastic raincoat he kept in his desk drawer and went down to the van. At close range the violence of the dog's terror was frightening. The animal was whimpering like a caught pup, it was frothing and bleeding at the mouth and nose. When it saw Dick its eyes fixed his for just a moment before it smashed its head and body against the window.

Immediately then it disappeared into the rear of the van. Dick placed a hand on the passenger door. The dog hit the back doors. Dick pressed the handle. The passenger door opened. Quickly he slammed it. A second later the dog hit it at full force. Dick stepped back shaking. He was getting soaked. In fifteen or twenty minutes the storm would be over. He turned and walked back to the Arts Building. Larry would have to look after his own dog.

Safe in his office Dick watched the storm pass. The dog was out of sight now, probably in the back of the van licking its wounds. The clouds were sliding away, the sky was deep blue beyond, and the cars in the parking lot were glistening with a million points of light. Dick's eyes fell on a happy-looking couple crossing the lot. It was Jan and Larry, coming back from coffee. Larry was being exuberant, with large gestures. Jan was looking at him. Her head was held on one side, and she was smiling and laughing at whatever it was he was saying. When they reached the van, Larry did an exaggerated finger-to-the-lips pantomime and they both took a quick peek through the rear window. He then led her away towards the front of the van, where he put into operation a succession of elaborate delay tactics. It was nearly ten minutes that she lingered there, the two of them engaged in a complicated, lover-like, public dance of prolonged leave-taking. And then, when they finally parted— Jan really was walking back towards the Arts Building, Larry really had got into his van— and Dick was about to turn away from the window, Larry's square, anguished face popped above the van's roof and he called to her. But Jan must have already entered the building and not heard, because Larry stared after her only a few seconds before ducking back into the van and roaring out of the parking lot.

Dick made sure that the door of his office was open an inch. He then sat at his desk and moved paper around with trembling hands until he heard Jan come down the hall from the mail room and go into her office. On the ride home and at dinner she seemed distracted, as usual, but unnaturally happy. She had nothing to say about Larry. When Dick asked casually what he was like she looked quizzical and said, "You met him. You saw what he was like." Dick did not tell her that Larry had called to her. He did not want her to know that he had been watching.

The van was not in the lot the next day, or the next. Jan became worried. "That's funny," she said as they got into the car on the second day. "Larry told me he had to study all this week."

"Your Larry's a liar," Dick said.

The next day, by purest chance, Dick was outside Jan's office when her phone rang. He stopped to listen. It was Larry. Dick stepped into Jan's office and closed the door. "No," he said. "You will not talk to Larry." He took the receiver from Jan's hand and replaced it.

"Dick, what are you doing?"

"This whole thing has gone far enough."

"What whole thing?"

"I saw you, the whole rigmarole. You're my wife, Jan."

"What are you talking about?"

When the phone rang again Dick put his hand on the receiver so that Jan could not pick it up. When it rang a third time he lifted the receiver and said, "Larry, you little creep. Harass my wife again and I'll have you out of this university on your ass." The phone did not ring again.

There followed two and a half days of tension and talk, tension and talk. At the end of the third day Jan apologized for being "too friendly" with Larry, while Dick acknowledged that he had "possibly overreacted."

The following morning the van was back, but the dog was not visible in the front seat. Jan went directly to the rear window and made a visor with her hands. "He's here!" she called happily, and opened the doors.

The dog jumped down past her and trotted straight around the side of the van towards Dick. Its front legs were bandaged, it held its head to one side as if curious, and as it rose towards him, Dick could see its muzzle lifted off its yellow teeth in what looked like a crinkled smile.

THE COMFORT OF THINGS
AS THEY ARE

The first time Jeff came to the hospital as a worried parent he had to walk halfway around the block to find an entrance, and then it was the wrong one. In the weeks that followed he never did figure out the complex of buildings. He would assume that if a wall ran along next to him, flush to the sidewalk, it was part of the hospital. Sometimes there would be a big ventilation fan, a fire sprinkler hook-up sticking out by his knee, a deep generator hum from a subterranean vastness behind steel-meshed windows. Or, just above his head, he would see a houseplant on a sill through a dusty, mud-splattered window, the hang of the curtains broken by the sill, and think that on the other side of this wall somebody was lying sick—or was it only an office?

Inside the hospital he was more lost. He made his way by familiar details, not by understanding. Like a squirrel he always followed the same routes. But partial lighting at night and on holidays could easily throw him, and he would wander off down the wrong corridors, needing to ask. Sometimes in his anxiety about his daughter he would cross to the nearest window and stare out. He would be on the twelfth or fifteenth floor, but still able through the dirty, narrow window to see a great stretch of the city, and he would never know the direction he was facing or what he was looking at. He could not relate what he saw from the hospital to what he knew from having been out in those same streets. Often the view was vaguely familiar, but as if out of some habitual laziness he never tried to figure out why, exactly.

The first time Jeff went to the hospital was right after work

70

one evening in November. His wife Sharon had left a note saying that she had taken Connie there and would call as soon as she could. At first the note made him angry. Connie, who was two, had been sick the previous night, but Jeff was sure it was only a stomach flu; Sharon had overreacted again— Unless Connie had got worse. Hadn't he himself been worrying all along? Frightened, he was rereading the note, searching for clues, when Sharon called.

"They don't know what's wrong." Her voice was quick and high with stress, and it pressed down on *wrong*. "They want to do tests."

"Why? What happened?"

Sharon said that Connie had been eating her dinner when suddenly she gave a long, weird scream and went limp for almost fifteen minutes—

"Oh God—"

"She seems okay now. She says she's scared. They want her in for at least twenty-four hours."

"Overnight? Should I come and get you?"

"No! I'm not leaving her here alone!"

"Of course not—"

"You'll come and be here? I could use some support."

He said of course he would come, right away.

Probably from memory—she was good in a crisis— Sharon gave Jeff a long list of things that she and the baby would need, told him the wing and clinic number, said she loved him, and hung up. Not good himself in a crisis, he did not think to write anything down; it was as if there was no time. And as he put down the phone he was already trying to find a way out. Not out of going to the hospital but out of this having happened in the first place. He wanted it to have been a nightmare, a misunderstanding, even some kind of trick. If it was true, then he wanted it to be *nothing to have worried about after all*, and if that was not possible, then he

71

wanted it undone. Meanwhile he moved around the apartment like a man in shock. He had decided he should eat but no longer had any appetite, and he was not able to concentrate on the contents of the fridge long enough to decide what he could stomach. He kept leaving the fridge door open to wander away and do random preparatory things—wash his face, find Connie's Raggedy Ann, change his socks, clean his glasses, find something to take to read. He knew that if he tried to make a list and limit himself to sensible things in a rational order, he would only get lost, set off looking for a pen, forget what he was after, go for something else, forget that too, and so regress into decrements of searching that would be even more useless than what he was doing now.

Finally, knowing he had forgotten a third of Sharon's list, he left the apartment. In the cold street the buildings, the lights, the traffic, existed faraway and implacable beyond a barrier of fear. The walk to the hospital took twenty minutes, and he spent it blaming Sharon for having wanted a child. A hostage to fortune. What he had given when Connie was born. At the age of thirty-five, real life had begun for him. He had felt the world distanced like this by fear before, but it always had to do with things like writing an exam, speaking in public, losing a girlfriend. Yet none of these perfectly major crises imposed the weight that the illness of his daughter did. So why had he given in to Sharon? Was it knowing that he could not go on saying no to her and still keep her love? Was it growing up in a small town, where a man was supposed to have his own family? Was it the quiet pressure from his parents, because his father's retirement had made their lives a vacuum they wanted to fill with grandchildren? Was it the knowledge that some challenges are more real than others and—by no doubt faulty extension—that some lives are more real than others? Was it having lived once with a very neurotic woman and knowing, against all logic, that the real reason the relationship would not last forever was not, as she feared, that she was too crazy but that she had had her tubes tied? Whatever it was, he had acceded to Sharon's wishes, Connie had taken years to arrive—that had been another unexpected worry—but she had done so, was real, their lives had been altered inconceivably, and now this. He suspected that if Sharon had said no to a child then sooner or later he would have taken up the other side of the argument; in his heart he cursed her for doing this to his life.

Jeff entered the hospital by the wrong wing, through a door that seemed to be for staff only. An impassive East Indian almost swept his feet out from under him with the swing of a floor polisher. At the hub of four spoking corridors he took the wrong one, had to retrace his steps, was given misleading directions by a nurse, and waited a long time for a car after he finally managed to find the elevators. It arrived filled with people squeezed around a high metal bed with a tiny baby in it. The baby's eyes were open, its hands were going, and there was a plastic tube up its nose.

Sharon was leaning over a metal crib in a bright room containing about a dozen cribs. In five or six of them were babies or small children. Only a few parents were there. The rest of the people in the room were nurses. Several children were crying; one was screaming.

"How is she?" Jeff said, putting his hand on Sharon's back and kissing the side of her head.

"Jeff, I'm so glad you're here. She's still throwing up—"

"Oh dear." Jeff bent towards Connie. "Are you feelin' lousy, little girl? Are you feelin' crummy?"

Connie stared whitely past him.

"When she throws up it comes out her nose too," Sharon said. "The nurse says she's never seen that before."

"Oh God."

There was a glaziness in Connie's eyes. Her arms moved jerkily. The front of her outfit was stained with vomit.

"Did you bring her blue T-shirt," Sharon said.

"Christ, I forgot."

A nurse came over. She had sharp cheekbones, short glossy hair, impersonal eyes. "How's she doing?"

"She hasn't been sick again—" Sharon said. She was going through the bag to see what else Jeff had forgotten.

"You're the father?" the nurse said.

Jeff nodded.

"We're still waiting for a bed. It could be a little while." The nurse went away.

"How long is a little while?" Jeff asked Sharon.

"Ask the nurse. Didn't you bring *anything* for her to sleep in? Jesus, Jeff. Ask the nurse if they've got something."

The nurse did not know when a bed would be available. She gave him a small cotton gown with strings and armholes. When he handed it to Sharon she looked at it and said, half to herself, "This leaves her back bare. At least she's got her cotton vest—"

It was two hours and still no bed. "Can we have a private?" Jeff asked the nurse.

"No privates in this ward," the nurse replied as if the request were undemocratic. She was drawing blood from an arm while another nurse pinioned the crying child. "There are two, three, and four beds in a room. It all depends on what is available."

A doctor came, a resident. "Hello. My name is Dr. Ho." Dr. Ho seemed nervous. He kept swallowing at the wrong time, his smile slipping. "How is the little one?" he said, leaning into the crib to examine Connie's pupils.

"She's not herself," Sharon said. "Couldn't we get a room? If I could put her to bed—"

74

"Yes," said Dr. Ho, "as soon as something becomes available. Now, could you tell me—"

And Sharon told him what she had told Jeff, who now studied Dr. Ho's face for traces of significant reaction: alarm, concern, reassurance. There was nothing. Dr. Ho suggested that for the time being Sharon should put Connie down.

"She won't sleep here," Sharon said. "It's too noisy and bright."

"It would be worth trying," Dr. Ho said. "In the meanwhile." He went away.

Jeff sat with a hand on Sharon's knee as she rocked Connie. After a while the nurse brought a four ounce bottle of apple juice, saying, "She should drink this."

"She can't drink juice when she's throwing up!" Sharon said.

"She should try," the nurse said.

"Do you have any Coke?"

The nurse shook her head. "Only ginger ale."

"Sometimes she keeps down ginger ale."

The nurse went away. A few minutes later she came back with a bottle of clear liquid.

"What's this?" Sharon said.

"Water," the nurse replied. "We have no ginger ale."

"In this whole hospital you have no ginger ale? Jeff, go to one of the machines on the ground floor."

"I'll try another ward," the nurse said and went away.

Jeff rolled his eyes at Sharon about the nurse, but she was gazing straight ahead, her mouth trembling. A few minutes later Connie began to dry retch.

The nurse appeared with the ginger ale. "Give it slowly," she said.

Connie drank feverishly, screaming each time Sharon withdrew the nipple. "We'll give her an ounce and wait ten minutes," Sharon said. Immediately Connie threw up the ginger ale. Jeff went looking for paper towels and the nurse. "Ask her for a Gravol," Sharon said.

The nurse told Jeff she would have to check with the doctor about the Gravol.

When the nurse brought a Gravol for Connie, she reported that their bed was almost ready. A half hour later Connie had the crib next to the window in a small three-bed room. The crib just inside the door contained a child of about three with a long, upturned nose, crossed eyes, and a very narrow head. She lay on her side making a strange keening sound. She had thin brown legs and long feet in loose white socks. A plastic tube was fastened to her stomach. On a piece of brown tape stuck to the foot of her crib someone had printed her name: *Grace Prince*. The middle bed was empty. "Why did we wait so long if there were two empty beds," Sharon said. The nurse, a different one, a stooped young freckled woman with a thin nose and big glasses, did not reply. She was busy making Connie's crib. Up and down the ward children were crying. Sharon handed Connie to Jeff and quickly set about organizing the few things that he had brought. Connie lay limp against his shoulder. "Could we turn the lights off," Sharon said to the nurse. "I'm going to try to put her down. She's exhausted."

"There's another one coming in," the nurse said. "They'll just have to be turned on again."

Jeff was at the window staring out, not recognizing what he was looking at.

"But in the meantime she might go to sleep," Sharon said.

"It's up to you," the nurse replied. "Is she wet?"

"Yes, I'm going to change her." A part of Jeff's mind recognized a familiar edge in Sharon's voice, and he turned back to the room.

"Give me the wet diaper," the nurse said.

"Jeff—"

"Uh huh?" It was as if all energy had departed his body, flowed out into the dream of the cityscape. He marvelled that he was still on his feet.

"The lights?" Sharon said.

"Oh. Sure."

Jeff was sitting on a blue plastic chair in the corridor waiting for Sharon to emerge from putting down Connie when a nurse went into the room carrying a screaming baby about a year old, followed by an ugly, fierce-eyed woman eating steadily from a bag of taco chips. Wanting to cushion Sharon, Jeff followed the threesome into the room. The lights were again on full; Grace Prince was frothing and crying in sympathy with the screaming baby; the ugly woman was pacing up and down pushing taco chips into her mouth saying, "Goddammit fucking nurses make him stop it, fucking goddam hospital—" Sharon was rocking Connie who had also begun to cry. Sharon's eyes were closed.

Jeff knelt beside her. "This is a nightmare," he said.

She nodded, did not open her eyes.

"Can I get you anything?"

She shook her head.

Within half an hour the nurse had quieted the new baby, and the taco chip woman had put on her coat and gone home. The room was dark. Jeff paced the corridor waiting for Sharon to come out and tell him that Connie was asleep. A black woman holding a baby with the tiniest head that Jeff had ever seen was walking up and down. She looked devastated. The ward was quieter now.

A tall, shiny-headed Jewish-looking doctor breezed past Jeff with his white coat flying and entered Connie's room followed by the nurse with the big glasses. The light came on. When Jeff reached Connie's crib the doctor was saying, "When she cried there were no tears, right?"

"I don't remember," Sharon said. She was standing over

Connie's crib patting her back. Connie began to whimper. Sharon picked her up and held her, a hand on her back. "Can't you just let her sleep?"

The doctor pushed a finger against Connie's arm. "Is she keeping anything down," he said.

"No—"

The doctor turned to the nurse. "Think we'd better," he said.

"Better what?" Jeff asked.

The doctor glanced sharply at Jeff.

"The father," the nurse said, ducking her head like a ventriloquist.

"Sorry," the doctor told Jeff, extending his hand. "Dr. Caplan. Better put her on the I.V."

"*What?*"

"Oh please no!" Sharon cried. "She doesn't need that tonight. Can't you let her sleep?"

"Afraid she does," said Dr. Caplan. "The little ones dehydrate pretty fast. The I.V. is standard at times like this. The nurses will rig it up in five minutes. Then she can sleep. She'll sleep fine. And if she's sick again she won't keep losing water." Dr. Caplan turned to the nurse. "She got some Gravol, right?"

When the nurse shook her head, his eyebrows went up.

"Yes," Sharon said, her eyes closed. "Downstairs."

"Okey-doke," Dr. Caplan said and walked away. He was back in the doorway. "Keep an eye on her blood," he said to the nurse. "Every four. And her heart."

The nurse nodded, and he went away again. "Don't worry about the I.V.," the nurse said. "It's really standard." Fifteen minutes later she came back with another nurse, who looked about seventeen. This one had broad hips, a broad face, and a hundred filaments of red hair that stuck out from her hairline to make a cloud at her forehead. It was a friendly, harried effect. She smelled like chocolate. "OK. Just down the hall now, to the Treatment Room," she said.

In the Treatment Room they could not find a vein. "They keep *moving*," the nurse with the big glasses complained. Connie was screaming. They tried both feet and a hand. Each attempt was preceded by an elaborate taping of the limb to a small board wrapped in cheesecloth. "Why does she sweat so much?" the nurse with the big glasses muttered, sweating herself. "It keeps slipping. Go get Denise." All this while Connie continued to scream. She did not like being held down and having her veins violated. Ten minutes later Denise, a sensible nurse with blue eyes and a drastically turned up nose, arrived. "Hiya," she said and quickly set about trying to get the I.V. needle into Connie's hands. After twenty minutes Connie had begun to retch with terror, and Denise gave up. "Better get a resident," she said with a shrug. "Sorry," she murmured as she left. "Kid's got the movingest veins I ever saw." The chocolate-smelling nurse went to find a resident and the nurse with the big glasses to check on another child. Jeff and Sharon were alone with Connie for the first time in hours.

"Jeff, why don't we just leave," Sharon said. "This can't be good for her. She's terrified. She can always keep down ginger ale at home."

Now, Jeff believed himself to be as sensitive as his wife to the horror of what was happening to their daughter, but it would never, ever, have occurred to him to leave a hospital undischarged. He could not accept that she was suggesting an act of such childish rebellion. It made no sense to him to get on the wrong side of people who might be the only ones who could help. "The nurses are inexperienced," he said quietly. "The resident will do it. It's routine."

"She's so small," Sharon whispered.

"Please don't be sentimental, Sharon. It just makes every-

79

thing harder." Jeff looked at his watch. It was 12:20 in the morning.

The resident was a casual young Mediterranean-looking guy in a striped shirt, jeans, and sneakers. "Hi," he said to Jeff and Sharon and ran his knuckle gently along Connie's neck. "What's up, little girl?" he asked. Connie was still sobbing.

"We keep blowing her veins," the chocolate nurse said. "We just can't find anything good enough."

"Let's take a look here—" and Connie, screaming, was once more placed on her back while the doctor examined each of her purple, punctured feet. "This one should take the butterfly," he murmured.

"No way," said Denise, who had come back. "She'll never keep a butterfly in."

"You could be right."

Jeff made worried eyes at Sharon, but hers were once again closed. The side of her head was pressed against Connie's mouth, as if her ear could absorb the whole of the child's pain. "OK," the resident said eventually. "I think this here should do. If it doesn't we'll have to try something else." Five minutes later the something else had worked. "Hey, wow," he said happily. "It's nice to do *something* right for a change. I've been screwing up all night."

Soon Connie was back in her crib asleep, with her right leg taped to a board and a tube in her foot attached to a plastic bag of sugar fluid on a hook above a metal box displaying winking red numbers.

"You go home," Sharon said to Jeff. "I'll sleep here." There was a folded cot by the wall. "You'll come in the morning?"

He nodded. "You'll be OK?" he asked, guilty to be the one freed from this place.

She hugged him and kissed his mouth. "We'll be OK."

Like a sleepwalker Jeff passed out of the quiet hospital and through the cold city streets to the silent, empty apartment. When he saw Connie's new red tricycle in the front hall he wept as if she had died.

In the hospital Jeff had longed to be at home, but beyond the quiet of the apartment there was no reward or pleasure to justify such longing. At home he worried more, and the fear was ordinary and immediate—not a distancing but a column of ticklish weakness at his core. He had a beer and a shower and wanted only to sleep, but he was afraid of waking up in the early morning with the cold shock of knowing that Connie's illness and ordeal had not been all a dream, and he slept badly, restlessly, afraid to forget.

The next morning he called in to work sick and was on his way back to the hospital by eight o'clock. It was a clear, windy day, and the streets were busy. He was tired but felt more able to deal with the situation than he had last night. He could imagine the end of the business. He could see the hospital as a separate place to which you could come and go. They had said twenty-four hours for the tests. He had hope.

As Jeff entered the hospital, the size and smell, the undeniableness of the place, brought the fear back. Waiting for the elevator with a slouching orderly, a bantering group of nurses, and various nervous parents and visitors, he could not pretend that he was not, like all of them, here because things really do go seriously wrong. Inside the hospital, implicated among these people, it seemed possible to him that his daughter might not be one of the lucky ones.

But the room itself was sunny and neat, and last night's anxieties faded in the bright cleanliness of morning and his wife's competence. Inside the door Grace Prince was lying in her crib on her side, frothing at the mouth. A small TV on an adjustable arm was placed a few feet from her crossed eyes. The taco chip woman, angry and pale, was rocking her baby beside his crib. She stared at Jeff when he gave her a smile, and he imagined her doing Sharon and Connie harm in the night. Sharon's end of the small room was tidy, and she and Connie were not there.

"Do you know where they are?" Jeff asked the taco chip woman. She shook her head without looking at him. Back out in the corridor the nursing shift had changed completely. Finally he found a nurse who learned from another nurse that his daughter was on the second floor having an E.E.G. He knew the room before he read the number because he heard Connie screaming when he came through the swinging door into the corridor. She was sitting up on a table wearing a yellow-stained straitjacket, being held by Sharon and two nurses. Sharon's hair was filled with vomit. Connie's head was covered with red Xs and gobs of a white substance like plaster of Paris. About a dozen wires led from her skull to a grey box with a swinging needle. The box was producing a read-out. "It's all right, Sweetie," Sharon was saying, over and over. To Jeff she looked as though she had hardly slept. When she saw him she held his eyes as she continued to try to comfort their hysterical daughter.

Afterwards, on their way to the elevators, with Connie once again limp against Sharon's shoulder and Jeff trying to maneuver the I.V. unit, which was like a coatrack on wheels, Sharon told him about the night that she and Connie had just spent. The nurses had done a blood test on Connie every four hours. They used a little thing called a lancet to prick her fingers, and it obviously hurt her; she wasn't just fighting having her arms restrained for the three or four minutes it took to get enough blood. Otherwise the nurses were in and out all night, taking the three children's temperatures, checking their hearts, chests, lungs, changing Grace Prince's diaper, attending to the taco chip woman's child when he cried, which he did much of the night, joined each time by Grace

Prince, who seemed to be in a state of constant ecstatic sympathy with all the ward's pain. And then there were the events outside the room. Babies arriving in states of fear and fever; older children lying in darkened cribs wailing with loneliness; single screams of anguish or nightmare that triggered others. Between all this and listening for Connie to retch, Sharon had not slept at all.

The morning had been worse. The nurse brought Connie a breakfast of bacon, a boiled egg, toast, and milk. "She's been throwing up," Sharon had said. "She can't eat this."

"I'm afraid she'll have to try to eat," the nurse had replied.

With difficulty and a long delay Sharon got the breakfast altered to apple juice and dry toast. Connie had just thrown up both the toast and juice in the E.E.G room, where Sharon had asked for more Gravol and had not yet been given any.

Back in the room, Grace Prince was asleep in front of her TV, dried foam around her chin. The taco chip woman had placed her child in a highchair. He was a big, ugly baby with his mother's furious stare. He gulped down the food like an animal and screamed when it was slow to reach his mouth. "Ask the nurse for some Gravol," Sharon said to Jeff. "I'm going to try to put her down. She's exhausted."

Jeff ran into a nurse on her way to a crying child and asked her for a Gravol. Ten minutes later Connie was retching again. "Why don't they bring the Gravol," Sharon said. Another nurse, who was pregnant, came in. She knew nothing about the request for a Gravol. She would have to ask the doctor. After twenty minutes she was back. "Do you have the Gravol," Sharon said.

"No, we're paging the doctor now. It's pretty early. He's not usually here before ten."

"Which doctor is it?" Jeff asked.

"I'm not sure which one is on this morning," the pregnant nurse said.

"For God's sake," Sharon said. "It's just a Gravol! You don't need a prescription."

"I'm sorry," the nurse said and brightened. "Well, anyways, time for our blood test."

"Again?" Sharon cried. "She had one two and a half hours ago."

"Uh huh. The lab closes for an hour for breakfast, so we have to do the morning one a little early." Connie had been watching the lancet in the nurse's hand. Her eyes were now blinking uncontrollably and her free foot was trying for traction against Sharon's leg. She threw her arms up and tried to wriggle out of Sharon's grasp. "It's just a prick," the pregnant nurse said, advancing. "Could Daddy hold your arm."

Jeff and Sharon held their daughter while the nurse jabbed the end of her middle finger with a three millimetre lancet. Connie jumped and shrieked when the thing went in. It seemed to take forever for the nurse to fill the little vial she needed. Connie screamed throughout. "All done," the nurse said. "What a brave girl. Would you like a bandaid?"

"She doesn't like bandaids," Jeff said. "They scare her."

"Oh, she'll have to have a bandaid," the nurse said. "You've got to stop the bleeding."

"The bleeding will stop," Jeff said, "if I squeeze it with a bit of gauze. Do you have some gauze?" The nurse went away for some gauze. While she was gone Jeff pressed a Kleenex against Connie's finger. Connie did not like having her jabbed finger pressed. The nurse returned with the gauze. "Oh, you found something," she said. "Here's a bandaid anyway, if you need it." She stripped the bandaid and stuck one end to the crib. She went away.

"I want to take her home," Sharon said quietly.

"Today," Jeff said quickly. "Probably this afternoon. Twenty-four hours."

"One of the nurses said a week."

"*What?*"

"She heard one of the doctors mention it. She thought we'd been told. They don't know what's wrong. There are kids in this ward with flus and chest colds. If she's not sick now she'll get sicker if she stays."

"But what if it's serious?"

"Then we'll bring her back."

"Maybe the nurse is wrong. These nurses don't seem to know anything. We have to talk to a doctor."

"It'll be too late," Sharon said in a distracted way, as if she were too tired to do more than repeat what she had mentally rehearsed.

"No. We'll tell him everything," Jeff said. "We'll tell him we see no reason not to leave unless he can give us a good reason for doing this to us. Fuck them."

A doctor they had never seen before entered the room. He looked like a slightly dessicated and unhappy Santa Claus, as if life had turned out somewhat more harrowing than he had expected. "Dr. Farr," he said, extending his hand. As Jeff said his own name he wondered uneasily if Dr. Farr had heard him say *Fuck them.* "OK," said Dr. Farr, addressing Jeff after he had shaken Sharon's hand. "Here's what's happening. We'd like to keep her for a few more days. Do a few more tests."

"What kind of tests?" Jeff asked. "What's the problem?"

"Oh, various tests. Nothing too unusual. We don't know what the heck the problem is, or if there is one at all."

"You don't have any ideas?" Jeff asked.

"Well, we know what you've told us, and that suggests we ought to check out a few things before we let you go."

"But when we came in they said twenty-four hours. Have you found something that should make it longer?"

"These things normally involve a few days. Sometimes it

takes twenty-four hours to get the results on one test alone. Sometimes forty-eight."

"Well, what *kinds* of things does what we've told you seem to indicate?"

"Oh, at this point I couldn't even begin to guess. As I say, it's probably nothing, but we want to be sure. More information is what we need. So—You realize you're welcome to sleep here?"

"Welcome?" Sharon said.

Dr. Farr glanced at her and back to Jeff.

"My wife stayed here last night," Jeff told him. "She didn't get any sleep. Neither did the baby."

"It can be pretty hectic around here sometimes, I know."

"It's not healthy here," Jeff said.

Dr. Farr frowned. "What do you mean?"

Jeff repeated what Sharon had told him about the kids with flus and colds.

"No," Dr. Farr said. "This is primarily a metabolism ward. Kids with respiratory, circulatory, and digestive problems. That kind of thing. We try to keep the contagious cases downstairs, and in any event always out of the same room. If she picks something up—and I'm not saying it's not possible—it'll be from somewhere else in the hospital." His beeper sounded, startling Connie, who was dozing against Sharon's shoulder. He switched it off. "OK? I've got to get to a phone. I'll let you know the instant we have something definite. I know hospitals aren't the greatest places in the world, but just remember we're here to help your daughter and we're doing the best that we can."

"Can she have some Gravol," Sharon said.

"Gravol?" said Dr. Farr. "Sure. No problem about Gravol."

"Bastard," Sharon said when he had gone.

"He seemed OK," Jeff said. "I mean his personality."

When Sharon didn't reply, he added, "Otherwise he's just a doctor, I guess," and looked at the back of the head of the taco chip woman, who had been listening. "I'll stay here tonight," he said, thinking that Sharon would refuse this offer.

But Sharon nodded and said, "I'm not much use to her like this. *Shit.* We didn't ask about the blood tests."

"I'll catch him," Jeff said.

"Get a Gravol from the nurse."

As Jeff went to find the nurse he was relieved that at least Dr. Farr's visit seemed to have reconciled Sharon to giving the hospital a chance. The nurse said that she would have to ask the doctor about a Gravol, but Jeff managed to convince her that the doctor had said it was all right. He returned to the room with a sense that science knew what it was doing in its sphere and that he and Sharon could effectively shield Connie from its harshest effects in their sphere. When the nurse came with the Gravol she said that Dr. Farr must have left the hospital; he was not answering his pager.

That night Jeff slept on a mattress on the floor beside his daughter's crib. Sharon offered him the folding cot that she had used, but it was too soft. After Sharon had put Connie down and gone home, he learned that Connie's blood tests were to continue every four hours for at least another twenty-four because they seemed "a little uneven."

"Meaning what?" Jeff had asked the resident who told him this.

"Nothing, probably. Dr. Farr just wants to see if a pattern develops."

"What kind of a pattern?"

But both the resident and Jeff knew that Jeff was being difficult. "It's sort of complicated to explain," the resident said without irritation, and Jeff let it go.

At midnight Jeff got up to restrain his daughter while the nurse, a new one, whose face in the dark room Jeff never really saw, pricked Connie's finger with a lancet and drained a few milligrams of blood into a narrow-mouthed plastic vial. The pricking hurt Connie, who cried and fought it with all her strength. She did not like being so cruelly awakened, and she did not like being restrained. The nurse seemed nervous and not to know how to take a blood sample from a child. She kept squeezing the little finger until the flow stopped altogether and she had to prick it again. In fact, she had to prick Connie's finger three separate times. Each prick sent a jolt through the child's body. Five minutes after the blood-taking was finished, Connie threw up. Supporting her on her hands and knees, gazing at the back of her small head as she retched again and again, Jeff wept. The rest of the night he lay on his mattress listening for signs of her vomiting again and waiting for the four, and then the eight o'clock return of the nurse. On those occasions he insisted on doing his own pricking of his daughter's finger and got the blood sample more quickly and with one prick. But from midnight on, Connie was too tired and frightened to go properly back to sleep, and like him was restless all night. Grace Prince and the taco chip child were mainly quiet through the night, except that Grace Prince cried in instant sympathy with Connie at midnight, four, and eight o'clock. Otherwise it seemed to be a quiet night on the ward. There were only the three different nurses in and out of the room every half hour.

In the morning a new nurse, smiling, Chinese, brought Connie a poached egg, sausages and canned fruit cocktail for breakfast. By the time Jeff had got this altered to ginger ale and dry toast, Sharon was back, looking somewhat restored. "You didn't sleep," was the first thing she said. "Go home and rest. Maybe you could relieve me for a few hours this afternoon. I'll stay tonight."

The hospital routine went on for four days, then a week, then ten days. Jeff had to go back to work, so he slept over Thursday, Friday, Saturday, to give Sharon a chance for a rest. After a week of hospital life the routine was grim but at least familiar. Jeff and Sharon hardly saw each other; sometimes they would spend half an hour together in the hospital caféteria. Jeff felt capable on the days after he had slept at home, exhausted and vulnerable on the ones after a night at the hospital. On bad days he looked forward to a night's sleep in the quiet apartment, on good ones he felt strong enough to endure another hospital night. The blood tests had continued, and Connie was now quite traumatized by them—"No needo, Mummy Daddy," she would say. "P'ease no needo." The vomiting had continued, but the doctors decided it was only in nervous reaction to the finger-piercing, and so they took her off the I.V. for a few days, but she must have picked up another virus in the hospital because the next day she was back on it, and that time the nurses found it no easier to find veins that did not keep blowing. Also, Connie now had a constant brain monitoring device attached to her skull and could not move freely. She was exhausted, frightened, and susceptible to severe and continued bouts of vomiting that left her white-faced, gaping, clinging, and grey around her staring eyes. On the fifth day she had shrieked and gone limp again, and again on the eighth. After ten days of testing, the doctors were still not saying what they thought it might be; it was as if either it was too terrible to be revealed without absolute certainty or they had no idea at all.

The worst part, of course, was not knowing. For Jeff the next worst was sleeping at home and waking up at three or four a.m. in a state of galloping fear. Compared to those terrible awakenings, the hospital and the punishing routine it exacted was a comfort. It was something that he and Sharon could actively endure; fate had afflicted them with this labour, this ordeal, and they would see it through. They told each other they were not like the parents who used the hospital to dump their kids or visited for an hour every three days, telling the sick one when they left that they were going to the washroom. He and Sharon were people who could face reality, could take hope and courage in the experience of their own daily powers of rejuvenation, of accommodation.

On the eleventh night Jeff was on, and Connie threw up again after her blood test. A resident who happened to come in saw what she had thrown up and asked when she had last eaten. When Jeff told her that Connie's last solid meal had been lunch, the resident seemed very surprised. For two hours Jeff lay on his mattress on the floor thinking how cold Connie's hands and feet had been lately, and he imagined her stomach gradually failing to digest, her whole metabolism slowing to a stop. As he lay there it seemed to him likely that his daughter was very, very ill. It seemed to him that the little girl restless in the crib a few feet away, his own flesh, simply might not survive. This thought came on the crest of such a wave of fear that Jeff's body seemed to become that wave, which rolled from his dissolving feet to the top of his dissolving head and on into nothingness, leaving only his thoughts, stripped down and working to find a way out.

When he could stand these thoughts no longer, Jeff got a nurse to call down to the night doctor in Metabolism, who responded to Jeff's scared questions about Connie's digestion in a slow, sleep-drugged voice, telling him that kids' digestive systems, like their circulatory systems, work in mysterious ways, and it was nothing to worry about, not, certainly, in the middle of the night. Tomorrow maybe Jeff might want to mention it to the doctor in charge.

In the morning a Dr. Karim, whom neither Jeff nor Sharon had seen before—though to Jeff he resembled the man with the floor polisher who had almost knocked him over—took them into a little ward lounge like a waiting room and told them that the hospital had not quite as yet got hold of Connie's problem. Dr. Farr had thought for awhile it must be her heart, but in Dr. Karim's view it could as easily be some sort of neurological dysfunction.

"Does that mean the blood tests can stop?" was the first thing Sharon said.

"Blood tests?" Dr. Karim replied. "I can't think why they'd still be doing blood tests. Better ask Dr. Farr when you see him."

"She's terrified of them," Jeff said. "They make her throw up."

"That's funny. They don't hurt, you know."

"The hell they don't," Sharon said.

"They're using the Autolet?"

"The what?"

"The little spring-action gadget?"

"No."

"They're using *lancets*?"

Sharon nodded, her eyes glistening.

"Oh dear," Dr. Karim said, wiping his face with a big white handkerchief. "Oh dear. It's the funding, you know. Over the past three years, do you realize what our nursing turnover has become? 30 percent. It makes for bloody chaos."

"They didn't have to hurt her," Sharon said in wonder. She put her face in her hands.

"So what now," Jeff asked Dr. Karim.

"A few more days for tests."

"That'll be two weeks we've been in here!" Jeff cried.

"And it's two weeks too long, you don't have to tell me," said Dr. Karim. "But we've no choice. This is something we haven't as yet tracked down. The brain is a very complex organ. It may be nothing."

91

"Otherwise, is it serious?" Jeff asked.

Dr. Karim smiled sadly. "Everything to do with the heart and brain is serious," he said. "How serious in this case, we don't know. How treatable—if treatment should be necessary—we don't know."

"But what is it?"

"An irregularity of some kind—"

"Caused by what?"

"Oh, any number of things. It could be genetic, or a genetic predisposition, triggered by a virus. Or a toxin." Dr. Karim smiled sadly again. "Something in the air, the water." He shrugged. "It's a terribly polluted world we live in, as you must know."

After Dr. Karim had said some words of reassurance with no more substance than his prognosis, he walked Jeff and Sharon back to the door of Connie's room and left them. While Sharon checked Connie, who was sleeping, Jeff sat down in the rocking chair next to the crib. "At least they told us *something*," he said.

"That they don't know," Sharon said. "God, Jeff, this is intolerable. We're so completely in the dark. We don't know the first thing about what's really going on with Connie's body. We're at the mercy of a completely crazy institution. We're at the mercy of invisible fucking chromosomes or invisible fucking pollutants that are actually capable of doing something awful to our daughter's heart or brain. This is just not fair. Nobody is telling us anything."

"Nobody knows much," Jeff said. Sharon had begun to cry. Jeff stood beside his wife with an arm around her shoulder. "Sounds like no more blood tests, anyway, Honey."

"Ten days of needlessly hurting her every four hours," Sharon said. "The wrong lancet. Can you believe it."

No, Jeff could not believe it, not really. He walked over to the window and looked out. He told himself that Sharon was exaggerating. Probably the first four or five days had been justified, the lancet business the kind of minor mix-up that happens all the time in big institutions. He told himself that he really should be more vigilant, more defiant towards the power that the hospital now seemed to hold over the lives of himself and his family. And then he wished that the window would open, so he could lean out and listen to the roar of the city in the ineluctable mystery of its operation.

UNACCEPTABLE PEOPLE

JACK

The first thing I noticed about Cary Dean Griffith was his left hand, because it was stroking my wife's leg. It was a big hand with soft fingers and you could tell that somebody was being paid to take care of the nails. The tiny hairs on the back were silky and colourless, and the light played on them as the hand worked the flesh.

This was a black tie function at the home of a guy called Alan Ignatius: white broadloom, gold chandeliers, framed weed arrangements. The weed arrangements were the work of Alan's girlfriend Thomasina. She dried them and then she glazed them. They were what first caught my eye when I walked in. Second, the guards, like bouncers, in shiny suits; Ignatius made his money on both sides of the burglar alarm business, so he only trusted blue-jaws. Third, at the Steinway, the celebrated Brenda Popescue, my wife, with her magnificent smile. Fourth, that big soft hand.

Later I walked through French doors onto a vast lawn. I found a rack of croquet mallets out there and hit balls around. They make a nice click. By the time I came in, Brenda Popescue and Cary Dean Griffith were long gone.

Six weeks later I ran into my wife at a bar, and she did not look well. It came out that she had been left by Cary Dean, or the other way around—it was not clear. At closing I begged her to come back. I did this because I thought I was depressed without her, but in retrospect I would say that my life had slipped into a quiet recuperative trough and I was just bored.

It did not work out. Before it did not, we were sitting around drinking one night and I asked her about this Cary Dean Griffith because I had started to hear some funny things about him. In fact I had been hearing funny things about him for years, but it was only after he borrowed her that I started to put them together.

Brenda thought for a couple of minutes and said, "Jack? You know the saddest single thing Cary ever said to me?"

"No, what?"

I stood up, my hand out for her glass, which was empty.

"He said his father told him that a man should have a goal, but he never told him what it should be."

"That is sad."

"Now, somebody like you, Jack—" Brenda rolled up her eyes to show me how carefully she was framing the delicate point she would make next. I flopped down on the chesterfield and spread my arms along the back to show her I was waiting. "You don't think anything about things your father told you, do you?"

"*My* father? No. Would you?"

"I didn't think you did." Brenda had her chin on her knees and was hugging them, rocking a little.

BRENDA

Hey Jack, got a minute? Story of my life.

When I was little we lived up north and mostly I remember my mother depressed all the time. She missed the big city, which was funny because she'd never lived there. She used to sit in the kitchen and smoke and talk and not clear her throat until you shouted at her to clear it. Swing or be-bop low on the radio, badly tuned in. One day I came in from school and she was sitting at the kitchen table with two scraps of paper in front of her, and each one had a signature on it, her maiden

95

and her married. *Frances Lewalski*: big loops, real energy. *Mrs. Lorne Popescue*: the capitals jerky, the rest levelled out like a terminal E.E.G.

She was the tired one, but it was Dad doing Dagwood on the chesterfield. On weekends they'd drink and fight, and sooner or later she'd call him a nothing. But she was the nothing in that little town. He'd lived there all his life, and she was too good for it. Once we'd moved back there, Dad had no intention of leaving, except for a month in '58 when we were all going to pack up and move to Karachi. Big textile management opportunities. Dad had hit it off with a Mr. Goona.

Nine years old, I was a little nervous.

"What kind of blackboards will they have there, Mum?"

"Stone."

So they'd have these fights, and the one who'd walk out was always her. Down the drive, left turn at the street, right turn at the highway. From the bathroom window I'd watch her march along the shoulder and disappear behind the trees. Headed south.

I was twenty before I noticed an interesting thing: She never took me.

My father'd be out in the backyard having a smoke. Then I'd hear,

"Brenda. Get in the car."

He'd wrestle her off the shoulder and into the backseat with me. I was there so she could stay for my sake. I didn't have to do anything. She never made a fuss over me. He'd chauffeur us back home, everybody dry-eyed and staring straight ahead. Every once in a while she'd scream into the rearview at him.

She died up there. Old swing, you don't tune it in right it breaks down the immune system.

JACK

Cary Dean Griffith, who borrowed my wife, had a droop in his right eye and big soft ears like acoustic guitar bodies. He was six foot three. He had swept-back blond hair with waves. When he got excited it fell forward over his face in ringlets, like Jerry Lee Lewis. He wore turtlenecks with mohair sports jackets, and he wore the turtlenecks backwards when they got stained. He was a careful and expensive dresser but the messiest eater I ever saw. Five minutes after he'd finished a meal you could ask him what he'd eaten and he would tell you in meticulous detail, and yet it would be all down his front. If he wore a tie he would sometimes spear it and chew on it by accident. He ate a lot of meat and he liked it tender. But he would eat anything. I have sat with Carry Dean Griffith in diners and watched him eat the scabs off the threads on the Ketchup bottle. He always wore white shoes, even in winter, and he hated getting them dirty. He had Velcro flies in all his pants because he liked the sensation the great *ri-i-ii-ip* made in the men's room.

Here are three funny things I had heard about Cary Dean Griffith.

One, the biggest problem in his life was spending the interest on the interest. On family fur-trade money. And here I'd thought all that was over with the *coureurs de bois*.

Two, Cary Dean Griffith was a drinker who really did have the control we all pretend we do. Hours, days, weeks ahead he would plan major bouts, including quantities. Even at home, where his daily beverage was coconut *feni*—Goan mescal—I never saw him lose it.

Three, in an expensive restaurant once he shot a porkchop; that's right: the chop was too tough, so he pulled out a .38 and shot it three times.

BRENDA

I never told you, Jack, once around the time Cary Dean was first in the picture I went to a marriage counselor about you and me. That was a laugh.

I arrived at the same time as this biker. He acted pissed off to see me there, and I thought he must be embarrassed to be seen in that situation by anybody. Right away I felt sorry for his wife, whoever she was. And then I thought, At least he's making an effort. But he went in a different door, and when he came out he had a sports jacket on and his hair slicked back, and this was the counselor.

What a duck. In his waiting room he'd set up a Christmas tree hung with construction-paper hands.

I asked him about it.

He ssp-ssps through his teeth and goes, "Friends' and clients'."

I go, "You're not getting mine."

After the session he tents his fingers and goes, "So. Think Jack could make it next time?"

"Jack? Make it *here*? Have you heard one single word I have said to you?"

One of the things I told him, Jack, with you I couldn't tell if it was the real thing or gratitude.

He goes, "Whose gratitude?"

"One guess."

"Yours?"

"Now why would you say a thing like that?"

"You didn't think you were worth loving?"

"Wrong."

And I explained that the reason I had lovers was to keep me so grateful to you for staying that *I* would.

I also told him my theory how if a man can convince a woman that her desires are his desires, then a hundred to one she will only want what he wants. This is what the world calls love. But sooner or later the truth creeps out, it always does, and that's why love never lasts, except as her little lie.

He asked me what I thought it might be about my own relationships that would encourage me to speak of all relationships this way.

I asked him why he didn't talk to me like an adult.

He goes, "I am talking to you like an adult."

I go, "You're talking to me like a demented child."

He goes, "What exactly is it about how I'm talking to you that makes you feel like a child?"

I go, "I'm not sure, but it could be the condefuckinscension."

He goes, "As a matter of fact, I happen to think you're a very intelligent woman."

"Yeah, well these things are relative."

By which time I know what he wants. Because I am intelligent, aren't I, Jack? A knockout too, right? What a good thing the clocks in here run the other way. Every day I'm more of a knockout. You should come and see me in here, Jack. Biggest knockout on the ward.

CARY DEAN

Jack Marquette's like one of those little guys with a beard who don't look at you while they're letting you know they know everything.

Jack hasn't got a beard and he's not too little. What he actually looks like is a high school teacher, the kind who don't look at you. He told me once he used to teach English to Chinese. One day a little into a class he noticed a message on his desk. It said,

"Your belt is engaged with your fly."

What could he do, he taught the class, all the time trying

99

to understand what this could mean. Afterwards he checked his belt, his fly, his shirt—nothing. He says he still wonders about it. Sometimes I'll lean over and say,

"Listen, Jack. As a friend, it's my duty to tell you. There's spinach on your teeth, there's shaving foam on your neck, and your belt is engaged with your fly."

He always laughs.

BRENDA

My real problems started when I saw *Wuthering Heights* and got my first period. I thought I'd ruptured from grief.

Twenty years later I took Cary Dean Griffith and he seemed to like it, but he fell asleep. Not that he didn't think we were soulmates or anything.

You say a man loves women and right away people go, Oh right, he hates them. But women are not so dumb, it doesn't have to be bad. In Cary's case it was bent out of shape by you, Jack. Cary recognizes your distance is purer than his. In his mind, you two boys are already halfway to the stars. Against a faith so strong a woman is either nothing or she's very important but useless, like a key he's picked up—but to what?

I don't think I ever told you, Jack, after the first time I took you to meet my mother, I called her.

She goes, "What's this got to do with me?"

I go, "You don't care who I marry?"

She goes, "Caring's not choosing, is it. You choose. Whether I care or not is my business."

She was a sweetheart, my mother. Shortly after, another visit, and on her mantle I notice these china figurines I gave her when I was a kid, a pair of elf ballerinas.

I go, "Wow, are these ever ugly."

Already she's crossing the room towards me. For a moment I'm five years old and she's going to belt me. When her hand comes up, I flinch.

But she goes, "I've waited twenty-five years for you to say that," and she picks up those little figurines in one hand and smashes them in the fireplace.

Hey Jack. Maybe this is less complicated than I thought. Maybe my old ma was too much for me, maybe I'm just like Cary, maybe I'm just like her. Maybe from people who are too much you learn to want to be with people who are too much. Maybe it's just one of the hazards of hanging around people who are too much.

Anyways, Jack. How do I miss you? The way my mother used to miss the big city. Badly. Without accuracy. Without any right. But you will visit me, won't you, Jack? Carry me along to the visitors' lounge and stick a cigarette in my mouth? Hold my hands?

CARY DEAN

Once I slipped LSD in Jack's rye. I know, I know. This was at my place, I took some too. An hour, two hours, nothing. Suddenly Jack jumps up and says he has to have a bath and he needs something to read. Well, I've got a whole wall of books in my den, floor to ceiling, and not all Nazi novels either. So while the bath is running Jack goes in there and comes out with maybe six. By this time I'm too damaged to understand what is happening. He stands there going through the books and finally he decides he'll put one back. When he comes out again he has more books, and less clothes on. This happens until he has twenty books in his arms and is completely naked. He's a stocky guy.

After that there's this period while my anxiety builds higher and higher, and it sounds exactly like splashing water. When the fish start climbing the drapes, I go see how Jack's making out. It's quite a journey, the kitchen's Future World, and so on. By the time I reach the bathroom, Jack's got the taps turned off. He's sitting in the tub, reading. Each page he turns, more water slops over the brim.

He says, "Where'd you get this?"

"The City pipes it in."

But he means the book. I have to ask what it is. The title's gnarled and writhing.

"*Wuthering Heights.*"

From Brenda. I tell him I don't remember.

He asks me if I've read it.

I tell him I tried, I couldn't get into it.

He says the bathwater feels like an element.

"Hot, eh?" I say. I dip my hand in, and I can't feel a thing. I look at my hand.

"Not hot," he says. "Fire's hot."

He's already back to his book. I stand there looking at him as if I'm waiting to be dismissed or something. And then he says,

"Fire's what the angels soak in."

Sure Jack. Anything you say.

So he reads all night. After awhile I make him get out of the tub and go to bed, the water's too cold. I sit up and drink and look out the window and think how you will be going along, things seem fine, everything's under control, and all of a sudden what happens? What have you got? Phrases. A few scraps of advice, floating. It's pitiful. I decide to go ask Jack if this is what people mean when they say the human condition. But I end up sounding *condition* over in my mind until it might as well be a chunk of the moon. And then the sun comes up and I can see every blade of grass in the city. What can I do, I stay with that, my green army. I talk to the troops.

Later I keep finding myself in the guest room, and Jack's still there, reading, on his side, with his head propped on his elbow. I swear he read that book cover to cover without moving, except when I made him move from the bath. By now I can't remember my question. Around noon he gets up, his whole left side is out of commission. So I help him get dressed, he's like a war veteran. By the time he leaves it's as if nothing's happened.

As he's going out the door, I say, "How was the book?"

And he says, "Unrealistic."

JACK

A week after Brenda and I had our one and only talk about Cary Dean, I flew out to the west coast, on short notice, to set up a club for a guy who called himself Bob S. Lee. Bob S. had payroll problems, it took a while, and I did not get around to calling. By the time I arrived back Brenda also had moved past all the crises into a sort of peace. But she was dead.

It happened two days after I got back, so I never saw her. Since nobody stepped forward to pay for her funeral, I sold the Plymouth. Who needs a car in a city like ours with its marvellous transit system?

Ten people came to the funeral, and none of them was Cary Dean Griffith. But afterwards we went to her favourite bar, and there he was, with that horse face, white shoes and mohair jacket, in a booth, in profile.

A few drinks and it could have been Happy Hour, but not for Cary Dean—who paid us no attention—and not for me. The others kept saying how they didn't know her all that well. This made me wonder. After eighteen years I sure knew certain old patterns she had with me, but as for a woman who once didn't have a pattern with me and, if she'd lived, one day wouldn't have one any more, I was lost. Another thing everybody kept saying was how she looked just like she was asleep, but whatever it was in that box it did not even look like the woman I knew dead. Why can't people get it through their heads that the point of a funeral, where you pay a man good money to make a corpse look like something made out of soap, is that the person is not asleep? There is a big difference between being asleep and being dead. People too dumb to recognize it should not be allowed at funerals.

CARY DEAN

One of the things about me and Jack, I can always make him laugh. Basically this is because I love the son of a bitch. You have to, because it's all uphill. I wouldn't call Jack moody, but I would call him a complex thinker. This can coil him pretty tight, and when he's coiled tight there's no give. Nobody's perfect, I'm not saying that. You love a friend as much for their faults as their good points. For me, friendship's friendship, straight down the line. It's an alliance in a cold world, against the powers of bullshit. Maybe I'm not such a great guy, maybe I'm the biggest scumbag on two legs. But I'll tell you, I never betrayed a friend.

JACK

I started to get to know Cary Dean the night of a party he threw at his penthouse around six months after Brenda's funeral.

The party was for a production of something Cary's friend at the time, Shirley Weston, the actress, was in. I remember half a dozen theatre types at the big picture window, making remarks. Cary kept turning the music up—it was his choice, it went with the decor—and then he disappeared and came back in these bright blue pajamas with dancing loons on them and threw everybody out, Shirley Weston included, but not me.

So there we were, Cary in his loon pajamas, an arm around my shoulder, drinking coconut *feni* from a crystal tumbler, me with a beer, standing at that picture window.

"Ever been up in Northern Ontario, Jack?"

"Never been north of North Bay, Cary."

I tend to lie when not completely at ease.

We were at the big window, looking out over the city. Twenty-third floor.

"Me, I grew up in Kapuskasing," he said.

"Nice name, Kapuskasing," I said. "Isn't there a big Kleenex plant in Kapuskasing?"

He smiled the way a person will smile at a fond memory and said, "Terrace Bay."

"Terrace Bay, right. I drove through Terrace Bay once—"

Whups.

There was a pause.

"Kapuskasing," he said, "is on the not-so-scenic route."

"Terrific scrub though."

"You go through Hearst, Kapuskasing, Cochrane, Kirkland Lake."

I nodded. Another pause.

He asked me if I remembered red Kleenex, and I said, "Hunters' Kleenex. The other drunk doesn't blow your head off because he hasn't confused that tissue in your hand with the ass of a white-tailed deer."

"Except," Cary said, "people looked at red Kleenex, thought *hemorrhage*, and put it straight back on the shelf."

We had a laugh about that.

We talked some more, and it was just talk. He told me about a bar he liked to go to for lunch where the tables are right next to the ramp and the girls will open themselves up in your face. He seemed impressed, the way a hick will be impressed. He mentioned the nice atmosphere in the place and the good-natured, relaxed girls who worked there. He said he would take me sometime. I said sure. For a long time he talked about the greyhounds, about how from one glance a dog expert will know how good the pedigree is, the way from one sip a wine-taster will know a fine wine. I think somebody in the greyhound business must have been snowing old Cary. We went on from there to something more interesting, what it was I don't remember, and then came this *thump, thump, thump*, and a woman in a white nightdress who I had never seen before hopped in from another room and shouted at him to stop drinking and come to bed. I thought she must have had one leg tied behind her back, but after she hopped out again, Cary Dean mentioned that Gloria never bothered to strap it on in the night.

I saw Cary a fair bit there for a period of two or three years. Mostly to go drinking. Sometimes we just sat around his place. He took me to that strip lunch place he liked, and though that was okay I did not become a regular. A teenage crotch in the face at noon can throw off my concentration all day. Maybe some old men get used to it. Evenings suited me better. Between us we knew half a dozen good bars. Also, Cary Dean knew a lot of people, though I did notice nobody's eyes exactly lit up when they saw him. As I said, he was never drunk, and yet he outdrank me every time. Some freak of chemistry—his body retained water, that's my guess. He was always hungry for a woman, had a lousy eye, was something of a moondog, the kind of man you could tell the younger ones were cruel about among themselves, giggling at secret jokes.

One night he asked me, "So what explains your success with the ladies, Jack?"

Warily, I said something about the importance of sensitivity to a woman's needs.

He put up his hand. "Bullshit like this, in other words. That's your big secret."

There was a story about Cary reacting to a shipment of *feni* that was short a crate by having his importer's borzoi strangled. Some of the women he went with, like One-legged Gloria, like Brenda, were fine. Others were spooks, and you had to wonder how he saw them. He liked to fight, and sometimes he would use women at parties to lure poor suckers in toe rubbers upstairs so he could ask them what the *hell* they thought they were doing with his girl. He was dangerous. But aside from the things that he actually did I could not see that he wanted to destroy himself. If you know what I mean. There is a certain kind of guy. One day he locks the garage and turns the key, and stuck under the windshield wiper there's a note that says, "Now you know what a jerk I really am." This was not Cary. Cary was a trying man. In both senses of that term.

CARY DEAN

Jack Marquette. I'd say the reason we've been friends for so long is the difference between us. It makes for sparks. A woman brought us together but no woman could ever pull us apart. Sounds pretty corny I know. We're hellraisers in the old style, Jack and me, the style that's not so popular any-more. Two buddies in a million.

JACK

Two years ago—he wasn't fifty—Cary Dean fell down on the sidewalk outside a bar. The police gathered him up, and it was eight hours before they figured out that he was not drunk. I went to see him in the hospital a couple of days after I heard. By that time he'd been in for a month. He was sitting by the window in a kind of games room with the sun full on him, and I did not recognize him. He was shrunken and grey.

His hair was cropped. The words he wanted to say were not the ones that came out. He was acting funny in other ways too, and then I understood what it was. He was embarrassed to see me. Over the next few months I called in six or seven times, not as often as I would have liked to and not as often as I could have. The only other visits he had were from Gloria, and hers tapered off. Later she told me she couldn't afford the massage she needed before she went so she wouldn't cry the whole time. Before she quit she rounded up clothes from the people who knew him—he wouldn't let her go to his place—and so in the hospital he was dressed in these polyester throwaways: check pants and plastic shoes. After a while his speech came back but in a way that made it hard to tell if he could still not find the words or if his personality had changed. For example, one day as I was leaving I said, "Hey Cary. Is there anything I can bring you, like a dirty magazine?"

"No, thank you, Jack," he said. He was facing me, but his eyes were fixed on a corner of the ceiling. He was talking slow like a phonograph running down. "That would not . . ."—I had to lean over and ask him to repeat the rest of it—"become me."

I looked into his face, and so help me I could not tell if he was kidding or what.

Next visit I brought him a twenty-dollar white hat, plantation style, for his walks outside.

As the weeks went by he complained more and more about the hospital. He was happy with the speech training but not the physical therapy, and he had the idea that the therapy would be better in the hospital up in Kirkland Lake and that was where he should be for treatment. I think he just wanted to go home.

CARY DEAN

My parents were always big party animals. They both died

108

young when you look at the statistics. But they expected that. Their parents had died in their sixties. Their friends died in their sixties. Everybody did. Anyways, they were partied out.

After Dad died my mother used to go over to her last living girlfriend's and watch the tube. At the time her girlfriend was dying of throat cancer, from the cigarettes and the booze. So they'd watch the soaps together and my mother would comb her girlfriend's hair, or what was left of it. One day, she told me, she was doing this when it had just been raining. Suddenly the sun came out. The doors onto the little balcony were open, and drops of rain were still coming down off the eaves, but the drops were clinging, the way they do, for a few seconds before they let go, and while they hung there each one shot out a rainbow, and as she was combing her girlfriend's hair my mother thought what a shame it was to go through the world with hardly a glance for the beauty of it, and what a waste they'd all made of their lives.

JACK

After Cary went back up north, he and I got together two or three times, on his trips down. Each time about a week before he came he would write to say he was on his way and we should get together "like the old days." Either he actually came only a couple of times, or he would call and I would be out, or he did not always call. I have eight or ten of those letters around someplace. Before he came he would run an ad in the personals, and both times I saw him he was with cheerful, overweight women. I could see that he was working to be his old self. He wore his own clothes. He was drinking again. The stroke had left his speech slurred, so now you could not tell when he was sober. He looked pretty much the same, but older, reduced. There was a kind of hesitation to his movements, and I know that since the stroke he was having some trouble with epilepsy, because he complained a lot that he wasn't supposed to drink on the medication they gave him for it.

"Not a problem, Cary," I told him. "You aren't supposed to drink after a stroke anyway."

He laughed, but then he had always considered me a great wit.

Somewhere recently I ran into one of his Personals dates, an obese woman in a banana pantsuit, and she told me how he'd had a seizure at a reception he took her to, and she went on about how embarrassing it had been. She meant for her, and I just walked away.

CARY DEAN

Just a note Jack to say long time no see and I will try to make it down next week or the week after. I will give you a call. I have had some health problems lately but the doctors say I will be A-OK if only I do what they tell me. Wouldn't you just know. Anyways I am being such a good lad you wouldn't know me. But I tell you Jack I live to get out of this place. Get out and see my old buddy again.

JACK

A month ago I got another letter from Cary saying he was coming to town and would call for sure. He sounded cheerful; the handwriting was steady and it was nearly spring. This time I was sure he would come. I didn't particularly want to see him, but I wanted him to be okay. A week later no call, and then I got a letter from him saying that he had not come after all because he had been sick. But the doctors had adjusted his medication, he was better now, and he would make it when he could. What a strange looking letter. It was as if he could not recover a downstroke with the pen; it was as if the whole letter was bleeding off the page.

Last week Cary walked out into a spring snowstorm. I talked to the orderly who found him, at a far edge of the grounds in a miner's squat, elbows on his knees, arms out straight, half a bottle of Triple Crown held loose in his left hand. He was dressed in some polyester outfit from his friends, my hat on, and he was gazing straight off into the bush, like a trapper enjoying a moment of perfect balance in the spring sun. There was snow to his waist, and the wind had made a little scoop in it around the base of the bottle.

In his will Cary left me ten thousand dollars and a scrap block of wood with a piece of glass nailed to it. He had the thing in his pocket when he died. One regular half-inch nail and three carpet tacks, each one driven straight in, no cracks in the glass. As if this was possible. A shoemaker in Montreal did it. Cary once told me how his father walked in off the street one day and gave the guy five dollars to watch.

I'm sitting here with a drink, holding this piece of wood and glass in my hands, and I'm wondering how anybody's touch could be so light. For ten dollars, Cary said, you could give the guy a lightbulb and he would hammer a half-inch nail into it. I can still hear the stubborn stupid awe and the hurt in Cary's voice as he insisted on the truth of this while I refused to believe it, for the simple reason that I was drinking and he wasn't producing any lightbulb with a nail in it.

And now I'm wishing Brenda was here to show this thing to, because either she'd say *Jesus* in a way that would let you know you only just thought you were impressed and how could you be so dumb. Or else, *Huh*, she'd say, *Neat*, and you'd know it was, there was no doubt about it, and all the folly between you and these people meant nothing, because in their own way they could see it exactly as clearly as you could. And like a drunk you'd be ready to give your life in the name of the neatness of the thing, and like a drunk you knew that the whole universe would stand behind you. Old Brenda had that kind of conviction to give, when she had it. And she had it to take away.

And then it's not a drink in front of me it's a mug of black coffee. Cary and I are still at some bar, in the back. If I open my eyes I can see him slung as close to the floor as I am, in a chair exactly the same colour as mine, drinking coconut *feni* from a crystal tumbler. His deep tan gives him the look of a man fresh-scorched by a blast of unhappiness. His long nose seems to be crushed and fallen, his eyes and ears and soft mouth are sagging.

Is he thinking she died from the same thing that had her with men like us? But how are we supposed to talk about that? Who are men like us?

"She was a wonderful woman, Jack."

He reaches out his big hand flat on the table and I look at it.

These foolish breaks in the wall.

Cary tells me, "Know what I am, Jack? A player. If I couldn't be a player I'd be a junkie."

Brenda Popescue and her magnificent, unconvincible lovers.

It never ends, it is never enough.

"A player at what game, Cary?"

He smiles with his long teeth.

"Life," he tells me. "Lived to the hilt."

Brenda looked thirty forever and she was beautiful, but she had a hard, hard mouth.

This adversary attraction. What is it instead of?

The light comes through and it's the wrong light. Pathos and sentiment has never made anybody a nice guy. It makes him do and say sad things.

I throw back my head and finish my drink.

These people come into your life and it is such chance and they are such a puzzle or such a drag that you almost think they are not really in your life at all. They are not people you feel you need to be other than yourself with; in fact you are a little surly about being no more than yourself, and so it ends up easy. Even though they are often boring or difficult, over the months or years you spend a lot of time with them because with them you do not have to worry about yourself. If it's a woman and she looks good enough you might even marry her. What I am saying is, you think you know these people better than you want to and you think you do not know them at all, but it is all the same. In the end it is a simple matter of a lack of regard, and it cuts both ways. They were the stuff of your life, and now they are nothing but memories, and not loving them is suddenly no protection against their pain.

YOUTH AND BEAUTY

Andrew and Nicky, nineteen and broke, were hitching to Naples. They sat against a stone wall in the shade of an ancient olive tree. They had been there since ten in the morning, five hours. There were few cars. Andrew did not know why they were going to Naples. He did not know how they could go anywhere without money. All he knew was Nicky's serene energy, her perfect beauty, her iron mysterious will.

"This one is slowing down," she said, brushing herself off.

Andrew looked and saw a horizontal strip of red metal shimmering in heat. It could have been a UFO. He hauled their knapsacks off the wall. When he turned he was looking down at a polished crimson Ferrari. A hand pushed open the door. Nicky held the front seat forward for Andrew to get into the back with the packs. The interior smelled of pomade.

"*Grazie*. I'm Nicky. My friend is Andrew."

The driver of the car nodded. His face was jowled and fleshy, the eyes half-closed as if the heat were pressing down on the lids. His hands around the wheel were tufted with hair.

"Nino," he said.

"We're trying to get to Naples," Nicky told him.

Nino nodded. "I will take you there."

"That would be wonderful," Nicky replied, reaching back to squeeze Andrew's ankle. Andrew shut his eyes.

Three kilometres down the road, Nino turned off.

"Where are we going?" Nicky asked.

"I must have clothes from my home," Nino replied. "Napoli is a long distance."

"Listen," said Andrew, coming forward. "You're not going just for us?"

"No, no. I must go to Napoli."

"How long will you be?" Nicky asked.

"Half an hour. No more. Then we go to Napoli."

"We must be there tonight," Nicky lied.

Nino nodded.

Andrew sat back.

Nino lived on the third floor of a high-rise on the outskirts of the town. Andrew wanted to wait in the car, but Nicky was willing to go up. Nino advised him to bring the knapsacks.

"They'll be okay," Andrew replied. "It locks, doesn't it?"

"Not good," Nino said, and put them in the trunk.

The apartment was shining surfaces in glass, mahogany, marble. Glazed plaster. It was very cool.

"Where is your wife?" Nicky asked.

"I am not married. I live with my old mother. She is away, visiting." There was a look of hooded melancholy in Nino's eyes, in the slope of his shoulders.

Nicky slid open a glass door to a small balcony. "We'll wait out here." Andrew followed her, shutting the door behind him.

Nicky leaned over the railing. There were dry fields stained purple with wildflowers; beyond, in a haze of heat, the edge of an industrial park. Andrew glanced around at the balcony door and saw Nino close to the glass, staring at the backs of Nicky's legs. He leaned against the railing next to her.

"Nino's a heavy breather," he said.

"I can handle Nino."

"Nicky, this isn't a contest. If he's not going to get us to Naples—"

"What is there for us in Naples. What money do we have." Nicky gazed off to the right. "Nino's worth at least a meal. He loves it."

"Loves what?"

Nicky laughed. "Youth and beauty, of course."

It was very hot on the balcony. Andrew tried the door. "The bastard's locked us out here!" He cupped his hands at the glass.

Nicky pounded on the door. She shouted Nino's name until he appeared.

"We were locked out," Nicky said, stepping past him into the living room.

Nino was wearing a beige dressing gown over a black shirt and a pair of light-coloured wool trousers.

"Look," he said to Andrew, pointing to some part of the sliding door. "You must not push switch."

Andrew paid no attention. "Are we ready to go now?"

Nino turned to Nicky. "Napoli is a long distance," he said. "We must have shower. Then I take you to my restaurant, where we eat. Then we go to Napoli."

"We have no money," Nicky said, smiling.

"No, no," Nino said. "Of course I pay."

"We will go to Naples tonight," Nicky said, "after we eat."

"Yes, yes."

While Nicky showered, Nino pressed upon Andrew a *Kama Sutra* picturebook and a box of chocolates. A few minutes later Andrew stepped into the hallway to see Nino crouched in the light from the frosted glass of the bathroom door. Andrew came out from his own shower to hear Nino begging for *un bacio, per favore, una sola volta, un bacio*, while Nicky stood hipshot in his mother's bathrobe, flipping through the *Kama Sutra* with an amused smile on her face.

An hour later, at the restaurant, a club called La Bagatella, Nino received an effusive welcome from the waiter, who showed them to a small private room, where Nicky asked for menus. There were no menus. The waiter and Nino discussed food in Italian. When the waiter went away, Nino told Nicky that he had ordered pasta with clam sauce and a main dish with veal. "Good," she said, and laughed. The waiter brought a bottle of wine. Nino filled their glasses and proposed a toast to "*la bella donna olandese.*" Andrew lifted his glass like a fool.

As they drank, and Nicky and Nino talked, Nino's breathing seemed to become more and more laboured, as if the alcohol were constricting his throat. When Nicky told him that Andrew was Canadian, he went into a confused story about how in the war he had killed nine Canadians. Shortly after that Nicky excused herself, and Nino grew confidential with Andrew, explaining with surprising precision how simple it would be to smash his nose. Not long after Nicky returned, a tired, sandy-haired man in a brown overcoat came in, shook hands with Nino, and pulled up a chair.

Nicky told the tired man that they wanted their knapsacks from Nino's car because they would like to leave now. When Nino expressed surprise at this, Nicky said she did not like the way he had been talking.

"What did Nino say?" the man asked her.

"My friend is Canadian," Nicky said. "Nino is telling us how many Canadians he has killed."

"In the war!" Nino cried as if exasperated, but his eyes were quite dead.

"This is not your husband?" the man said.

"We are engaged," Nicky replied.

The man smiled at her. "Saving for a ring." He nodded towards Nino. "Nino is a good man."

"I am sure he is," Nicky said. "But we would like to go. We must get to Naples tonight."

"It is too late to go to Napoli," the man said.

Nicky shrugged. "We must."

"Tonight you should stay here, in a hotel."

"We have no money."

"Ah. And no money in Napoli."

"There is money waiting for us in Naples."

"*All'angolo della strada?*" the man said, with a glance at Nino.

"In a bank," Nicky replied.

"Tomorrow."

"They stay with me," Nino said.

"We do not want to stay with him," Nicky told the man. "We want to go. We have done nothing wrong."

"They must pay for food," Nino insisted with sudden passion.

"Nino told us he would pay," Nicky said.

The man shrugged. He smiled at Nicky. "Then you must eat," he said. He said something to Nino, who closed his eyes and nodded. "Nino will pay. If you eat."

"And then we can go."

"*Naturalmente.*"

"*Grazie.*"

The man bowed slightly, where he sat.

As if the waiter had been waiting only for this conversation to end, the food came. There was a great deal of it. Andrew was not hungry. Nino ate doggedly; swallowing seemed to interfere with his breathing. Nicky mopped her plate clean with bread.

The tired man, who was chief of police, amused himself during this meal by asking Nicky questions about her life and travels. An interrogation based on assumptions of female guile, lust, helplessness. Nicky answered his questions with perfect good humour. When the three had finished eating and the last of the wine had been drunk, she smiled at the chief of police and said, "Now then. May we go?"

In reply he raised both hands in a gesture that said they had been free to leave all along, or perhaps it said the matter had nothing to do with him.

"May we get our packs?" Nicky asked Nino, who answered with an expressive shrug. At that moment Andrew found him almost likable.

But when they got out to Nino's car, it seemed that he had taken their knapsacks up to his apartment after all.

"More safe that way," he explained. "We go back and you get."

"Come with us?" Nicky asked of the chief of police.

"No. Nino is a good man. I will wait here."

So Nicky and Andrew got back into Nino's Ferrari. On the way, Nino berated them in Italian and English for their foolish fears. He portrayed himself as an honourable and generous man. At a stop light he reached around to pinch and twist Andrew's cheek. In the apartment he made Nicky fold and put away his mother's bathrobe, and then get down on her knees to scour the tub. But he gave them their knapsacks, and he drove them back to the club, where the chief of police was waiting in his car. As they got out of Nino's car, Nicky said, "Thank you for dinner." Nino looked at her without expression.

Andrew followed Nicky over to the car of the chief of police. When she tapped on the glass he closed a paperback and wound down the window.

"I know Nino all my life," he said. "He is a very unhappy man. Women say he bothers them, but he is harmless. Get in. I will take you to a good, cheap hotel. Tomorrow you take the bus to Napoli. That is my advice to you. It is not a good town for you here."

The hotel was ten times more than they were able to afford. They walked three miles to a hostel, which cost them the rest of their money. They could just afford breakfast: hot chocolate and bread. Nicky stole a paper and studied the want ads.

"They need dancers at Nino's club," she said.

"It wasn't Nino's club."

"And a dishwasher."

"We'll fit right in."

"A month. How close are we to a beach here?"

"Water's just across the highway."

As they walked along the road to La Bagatella, a red Ferrari drove slowly past, without stopping.

Fear washed up and down Andrew's legs.

"Poor Nino," Nicky said.

Emilio, manager of La Bagatella, slammed through the swinging door to the kitchen. "*Canadese! Uno cucchiaino!*"

Andrew tossed him a spoon.

"Your girlfriend really knows how to pick them," Emilio told him in Italian, scooping butter from a plate on the staff table. "*Hi cuoco.*" He licked the spoon clean. "Guess who's buying *l'olandese* her champagne tonight."

"Marcello Mastroianni," said the cook, his back to Emilio.

"No, smart guy. Duke Cesare Federigo di Bondone."

"Who?" said the cook.

"Never mind. He's class. You wouldn't understand."

"What's he doing in this dump?" the cook wondered.

Now Emilio was looking worried, his little eyes pulled in close together, studying butter again. "I just hope to Christ she doesn't—"

At that moment the barman's head poked into the pass-through. "Hey Emilio. She's at it again."

"*Merda!*" cried Emilio, stabbing the spoon into the butter. "What did I just say?" He rushed over to Andrew. "Is she *greedy* or something? Doesn't she make enough on the booze Nino buys her? So help me I'll put the bitch on straight commission—" Emilio flashed his cuffs and slammed out through the swinging doors.

The cook looked around at Andrew, who returned his

gaze without expression. The cook shrugged and went back to buttering sixty-four slices of bread by dunking his hands in melted margarine. "If *l'olandese* wants drinking contests with patrons to top up what she makes on the drinks they buy her," he said, "then let her have drinking contests."

A half hour later Nicky stepped carefully into the kitchen as if balancing something invisible on her head. Andrew thought that she had won again. She was smiling. But she was very white, there was a glaze to her eyes, and when she tried to hug him she passed out in his arms. Later he was told she had fallen twice on her way to the kitchen. He carried her upstairs and put her to bed. Seeing her there on her back he saw her the first time they made love, her heels pressing the base of his spine, her hair spread against broadloom the colour of moonlight. For some reason—were they hiding?—they were down between a bed and a wall. The room was soft with dust. He remembered studying her face, her eyes closed and quivering, focussed on this extraction of pleasure. When it was over, she was not embarrassed, did not weep, talk tough, act drunk, fake remorse. She did not discreetly arch her back and slip him out. She looked him in the eyes and said, "You can do that again, when you like."

Next day Andrew said, "Nicky, let's get out of here."

"Now?" from under her pillow. "After losing?"

"You lost on purpose."

"Let Emilio think so. His Grace outdrank me. We can't leave now, my love. Too much justice to be served!"

"Nicky, why?"

She sat up, winced, eased herself back on the pillows. "Because I am learning and I am having fun and they fascinate me so much." Nicky laughed, then held her head in both hands and slid, moaning, under the comforter.

One morning she was not there when Andrew woke up. Later that afternoon they talked, in the roar of the dishwasher. Her eyes were glittering.

"You didn't come to bed last night."

"I went to the country with Cesare."

"Cesare."

"The duke, with the winery. Andrew, listen. You must make me a date with Nino. If Nino brings me to work tonight, Emilio won't fire me."

On the phone Nino's breathing grew heavy when he heard Nicky's name.

Upstairs she was standing in a white silk dress at the bathroom mirror, spreading make-up under her eyes.

"Nicky, what about me?"

Her eyes regarded Andrew from the mirror. "You have nothing to do with it. You love me. Cesare could be my father. He is fifty-seven years old. Vain, silly, charming, intelligent, impossible, foolish enough—just now—to give me anything I want." She smiled. "This is one it is my true destiny to improve, outwit, shame, and exploit."

"You're in love," Andrew said.

"I am still high on coke, and I have had no sleep. I have never been in love. Except with you."

Andrew turned from the mirror and sat down on the bed. Five minutes later Nicky kissed his cheek and left to meet Nino. When the door closed behind her he started to shake. An hour later he called down to the kitchen sick. This was because he could not stop shaking.

In the night the door was unlocked. A white shadow grew in the darkness in front of where Andrew huddled, half dreaming. "Nicky—?"

Her breathing was shallow. She collapsed before the bed. He groped towards the whiteness and pulled her up. Even in that darkness he could see the blood on her dress, the discoloration down the side of her face.

Emilio was hammering at the door. "Andrea! Let Nino speak to her! Only for a minute!"

Nicky shook her head.

"No! Go away!" Andrew shouted.

"I know she is there!" Emilio cried.

"She doesn't want to speak to Nino!"

"Then you must come!"

Nicky said something. Andrew had to ask her to repeat it. She said that Nino had raped her.

"I'll kill him," Andrew said and heard himself say it.

"No. Call the police."

"*Andrea!*"

"Send the bastard to jail," Nicky said.

"Emilio!" Andrew called. "I'll talk to Nino!"

"Don't—" Nicky said. "Don't trust them."

"We should trust the police?"

He rinsed his face in cold water and went to the door. Emilio looked terrified. "It is a misunderstanding," he said, taking the firestairs. "A case of seduction. She wanted it *rudivo*."

Andrew reached over Emilio's shoulder and lifted him into the air—he seemed so light—then swung him hard against the wall. "No, Emilio," he said. "She did not want it *rudivo*."

"Talk to Nino," Emilio whispered. The little eyes were all over the place.

"Say again she wanted it *rudivo* and I will kill you," Andrew said.

"I do not say it again," Emilio agreed.

"No, you do not."

Nino was in the office with the owner, the bouncer, a waiter, and several other men from the club. He stopped

123

talking when Andrew came in followed by Emilio. For a moment he studied Andrew's face. Then he said, "She said I must help her to keep her job. I said I will do this for you. What will you do for me—"

"You raped her, Nino," Andrew said and took a step forward. Every man in the room shifted his weight. "I'm calling the police," Andrew said.

Nino's hands came together in supplication. "No, you must not do that," he whispered, shaking his head. "You must not do that."

Andrew started back upstairs. Immediately Nino was at his back, breathing hard. Andrew turned and saw that he had taken out a handful of ten thousand lira notes. It was two inches thick. "I will pay you," Nino said. "She must not tell police." With imploring eyes he held the money at Andrew's face.

"What are you worried about, Nino," Andrew said. "The chief says you are a good man."

"I am a good man," Nino said, his eyes filling with tears. "*Mia mamma*. It will kill her."

Andrew started up the fire stairs, followed by the whole group. He took the stairs two and three at a time. Ten flights. His energy was boundless. He let himself into the apartment and locked the door. Nicky was still in the dark. He turned on the light at the door and went to the bathroom for a cloth. She was crouched in a corner of the bed like a beaten child. As he wiped her face, she whispered, "Did you phone the police?"

"He wants to give us money."

"Phone them."

"He says it'll kill his mother."

"His mother will live. Phone the police."

More hammering at the door. "Andrea!" called Emilio. "Let Nino speak to her! Only for a minute!"

124

"Don't let them in," Nicky said.

"*Andrea!*"

"Please," Nicky said. "I love you. *Please.*"

There was a key, loud, in the lock. "Stay out!" Andrew shouted.

"Only Nino!" Emilio called. "We leave!"

And around the partition came Nino. He was on his knees. He held the massive stack of bills in his left hand and a crucifix extended in his right. He came towards them still on his knees, his head wagging from side to side. Repeatedly he crossed himself, brought the crucifix to his lips.

"*Mia carissima mamma*," he wept. "It will kill her. Please. Forgive me. I am a good man—"

Nino reached the bed and grabbed hold of Andrew's sneaker. When Andrew kicked out at his face, Nino received the blow like something merited. The crucifix hung from his right hand as he peeled bills from the stack in his left and threw them onto the bed. Andrew kicked him again, in the chest. And again, in the side of the head. From each kick Nino recovered to throw down more bills. This went on until there were no more bills in Nino's hand. Money littered the bed. Nino was bleeding from the nose and forehead. His eyes were wild. Andrew kicked him again. Nino's hand went to his pocket. It reappeared with more money. The kicks continued. Nino was having difficulty staying on his knees. He leaned on an elbow, throwing down bills. After a long time he collapsed. Andrew stopped kicking, there was a silence, Nicky mumbled something. Andrew put his ear to her mouth.

"More," she said.

Nino heard and struggled to lift his face. Andrew kicked it. More bills fell from Nino's hand.

"More," Nicky said, distinctly.

Andrew kicked Nino again. More bills fell.

"More," Nicky said, louder. Her voice was hoarse, from deep in her throat.

When Nino collapsed, Nicky reached over and took from his hand what remained of the second fold of bills. She held the money to her chest. When Andrew dragged Nino into the hall, he trailed blood. The others were sitting on the firestairs, smoking and waiting. Andrew locked the door and chained it.

Then he went over to the bed and began to gather up the money. He knew they would have only a few hours between the time the men took Nino away and the time someone was sent back, but he believed they would make it. The thing was, he felt he could handle the situation.

"Hey Nicky, we're rich," he told her in a shaky voice.

"More," Nicky said.

THE MARY DUNBAR LETTER

Twenty years ago the British Library was still called the British Museum, and I was visiting the Students' Room of the Department of Manuscripts, reading through a stack of volumes of documents and autograph letters relating to Jonathan Swift's tenure as Vicar of Laracor. After three or four hours I found myself—as I always seem to be doing in the British Library—looking through a volume that had been delivered to my desk by mistake. This was a collection of mainly legal papers (d. 1703-11) from the office of a County Antrim puisne Justice of the Queen's Bench (and later, very briefly, of Common Pleas) named Anthony Upton. Dryasdust stuff, except for a series of depositions relating to a witchcraft trial that Upton and another judge presided over at Carrickfergus on 31 March 1711. But more interesting to me than the depositions was an autograph letter of six close-written pages that had been mounted, in error, in the volume along with the depositions, which at first glance it resembled. It was not, however, a deposition but a letter written—and apparently sent (it is dated the day after the trial)—to Judge Upton by Mary Dunbar, the woman whose experiences were the occasion of the trial.

I present the letter here as a sort of "found narrative," exactly as I copied it out in the Students' Room in November 1969, with only the spelling and, here and there, the punctuation regularized. In square brackets I have provided information gleaned from the depositions, as well as from various published accounts of these events and of the trial, and have inserted occasional words and affixes (also in square brackets) when I have thought I could make the sense less obscure.[1]

All Fools' Day

Sir:—

I entered service at the house of Reverend John Haltridge [Presbyterian minister in the parish of Island Magee, near Carrickfergus, County Antrim] on my fifteenth birthday nine years come May. Reverend Haltridge dying of a cancer, Mrs. Haltridge [i.e., his widow Anne] and myself went in the last week of September to stay at the house of her son, James Haltridge, also of Island Magee. There my mistress suffered grievance in the night for many nights from some thing, that threw clods and stones at her bed while she slept though the casement was not open. Many times the curtains [of her bed] was forced [open] by blows and three times they [? the blows] drew them all round. With my own eye I saw it, though invisible, snatch pillows from under her head and pull off her bedclothes entire. These it made to storm in the room until my mistress cried out. When the servants come in they [the bedclothes] fell down of a heap. But we seen it both. Mr. Haltridge made a close search but found naught. Two days after[wards] my mistress moved to another room and all annoyance ceased.

On 11th December my mistress was a-sitting in the evening by the kitchen fire when a small boy strut boldly in and squat on the hearthstone. As my mistress told me, he was twelve or eleven years, with black cropped hair, wearing a black bonnet on his head, a dirty vest, and a worn-out blanket that trailed the floor. His face he kept hid in this blanket. My mistress asked him questions: "Where he [had] come from? Where he was going? Was he cold or hungry? Would he have rest by the fire?" He did not answer but frisked round the kitchen then ran out [of] the house and disappeared in the cow-shed. I was fetched from my room and give chase with the servants by request of my mistress. We looked all about, [but] he was not to be seen. Yet Bess [the upstairs maid] returned to the kitchen and he was there. He had snatched a bit of mutton out of the fire and eat it snapping and snarling like a ravening beast. When she tried to catch him he run off. We looked again and he was nowhere to be found. At last Bess, spying the master's old dog trot in, cried out that Mr. Haltridge was come home and *he* would soon catch this vexsome creature (or some such words), whereupon he puffed into smoke before her eyes, or so she swore after. And indeed we were not much plagued by his company till February this year.

On the 11th, which was Sunday, my mistress was alone in the sitting room abovestairs reading Dr. Wedderburn's *Sermons on the Covenant*. When she lay the book to one side a short time it was suddenly took away. She looked for it all round her chair but could not discover it. On the day following he [the boy] thrust his hand through the windowpane of the scullery with the volume in it, telling Margaret [Spear, the kitchen maid] that this book my mistress would never see more. Margaret, seeking to detain him, asked if he could read it. To this he replied that he could, the Devil had taught him that wee trick and a hundred others beside. Hearing this, Margaret cried out, "The Lord bless me from thee! thou hast got ill lear [learning]!" He then let fly an oath and, drawing a sword, swore further that he would kill every Christian in the house. Margaret ran into the parlour and fastened the door, but the boy laughed at her and told her that the Devil had taught him to crawl through the smallest holes like a toad or mouse. Saying this, he took up a large stone and heave[d] it through the [parlour] window.

Somewhat after, we looked out and saw him seize the turkey-cock by the tail. He then threw it over his shoulder, the bird making great fuss with his feet so that the book was shook out of a knot in the blanket. Directly he leaped on the wall with the bird over his back he would draw his sword for to kill it but the bird escaped. Missing the book then, he ran nimbly up and down in the yard in search and then come with a club and broke 7 panes in the kitchen. We looked out and saw him in the yard, mining [i.e., digging] with his sword. Seeing us watching he said, "I am making a grave for a corpse which will soon come out of this house." He then flew over the wall as if he was a bird. When Mr. Haltridge, who had been away the while, come in, he examined the book, which pages was all bedaubed with dung.

For 3 days nothing. On the morning of the 15th the clothes was pulled off Mrs. Haltridge['s] bed and stuffed in a bundle behind. New being put on by me they was again took off, folded up and placed under a table that was in that room. A third time I made up the bed and this time they was put in the middle of the floor, shaped in the form of a corpse.

Now several gentlemen, believing a trick, come to inquire. Reverend [Robert] Sinclair [Presbyterian minister at Island Magee, successor to John Haltridge], with Mr. [John] Man and Mr. [Reynold] Leaths [church elders], stayed the next day and night, passing many hours in prayer. The night following [their departure], my mistress went to bed, but at midnight she cried out. Upon [my] going to her, she told me that a knife had been stuck in her neck. On the next day Mr. Haltridge put her in his room (for he and his wife kept separate chambers), himself moving into the room where she was first troubled. But the pain never left and at the end of that week, the 22nd [of] February, she died. All the time she lay ill I stayed at her bedside, and when I went out [of] the room (as from time to time I must) the clothes was took off her bed and shaped in the middle [? of the floor] like a corpse. Once I tied them to the [bed]posts with stout cord, but upon my return the knots was all undone and the clothes laid out like a corpse. The morning before my mistress died they was took off and folded with great care in an upstairs chest.

I was pleased then to be engaged by the daughter[-in-law] of my late mistress. When preparing her room on the 27th [of] February, I saw her new mantle, bodice, vest, stockings, and other fine apparel scattered upon the floor. In the parlour, meantime, Bess found an apron that I had locked up in a closet two days previous. The key was yet in my pocket. The apron was rolled tight in its strings, that had in them 7 knots. Bess, as I was told, found a flannel cap wrapped in the apron that my late mistress was fond of. After supper Mr. Haltridge called me to his study and says "I am a pretty lass but he must discharge me as the servants accuse me of working witchcraft in the house." "And before me they would blame the troubles on your own mother, I says." But he tells me only "hold my tongue" and give me my wages.

In my bed that night (for I would set out in the morning) a fit come over me. I saw and felt a knife run through my leg by a woman that I could not see. Margaret sat by me then and the fit soon passed, though scarce the burning. But at midnight 7 or 8 women seemed to crowd in, talking among themselves about how they would do me harm. "We will stick her all over with knives, says one." "No, cries another, we will tip boiling oil into her ear as she sleeps," etc. The boy was among them the while, and even as they argued, they caressed him most lewdly, showing their asses to enflame him. They called each other by their names, so when they left I names them to Margaret: *Janet Liston, Elizabeth Cellor, Kate M'Calmont, Janet Carson, Janet Mean* (who twisted my tongue, and with her bony fingers and swelled knuckles pressed it so I could scarce breathe and would tear out my throat if she could), one they called *Latimer*, and a sly one they called but *Mrs. Ann*. I also give a strict account to Mr. Haltridge, who spoke to Reverend Sinclair and to Mr. Man, who sent for women answering [to] those names and fitting my descriptions and others besides. As each one come near the house I fell in a fresh fit, though I could not see them approach. When they brought in [Janet] Carson [a seamstress] I felt a most cruel pain in my knee. After[wards] they looked and found a fillet belonging to my mistress tied fast about it with 7 double knots and one single. Mr. Adair [a local teacher] sent one [woman] and the fit come on again, driving a knife in my thigh, and when she come in I says, *O Latimer, Latimer* (which was her name) and she hit the description I give Margaret. In this way, out of 30 brought to me I found at first 7 true witches. This, however, made them wrath[ful] and they swore they would carry me out the window but I called out to God in my mind and they let me drop. I was told after I had rose off the bed and sunk all outstretched to the floor.

At this time they begun to put things in my stomach and I to vomit them out again, viz. feathers, yarn, wool, pins, waistcoat buttons (5), hair, clippings of nails, mouse claws, and suchlike. These caused terrible torments in my guts. Also at this time I had suffering by a woman blind of an eye who told me they would hinder me hearing the curate's prayers for me, which they did. Three women blind of an eye were brought and they did not bother me. But when they brought [Jane] Miller near the house (though I did not know it), I fell a-sweating and thought I should faint and when they brought her struggling in the house, I fell in such fits that two men said they could not hold me, and [I] cried out, "For Christ's sake, take the Devil out of the room!" This creature was possessed, for she says to me, "If the plague of God is on thee, then the plague of God be on us all together, and if the Devil is among us God help us all. If God has taken thy health then God give thee health; if the Devil has taken it, then the Devil give it thee." She then stares like a madwoman about the room and cries in a loud voice, "O misbelieving ones, eating and drinking damnation to yourselves, crucifying Christ afresh, and taking all out of the hands of the Devil!" I heard no more, being made senseless by this talk. They took her from me and charged her. After this fit they found string tied round my waist that was not there before, with 7 double knots and one single. Father O'Hare then advised Mr. Haltridge to write some words out of St. John. This paper Mrs. Haltridge would tie in an incle [i.e., length of narrow tape] knotted three times round my neck. The women [in my visions] refused, but in one of my fits she sneaked it on. I was then thrown in violent convulsions, being held down by three men, and a horrible pain struck through my middle. Seeking the trouble, Mrs. Haltridge discovered the incle tied now round my waist, with 7 double knots and one single, my hands being held fast the while.

On Sunday the 28th [of] February Mr. Haltridge would have them carry me to church to partake [of] the sacrament, but the women [in my visions] declared I would not go over [the] threshold of that chamber. Several times did the men attempt to lead me out but as often was I thrown in fits. They then took up the threshold but were immediately struck with a horrid stench of brimstone that reeled them back and spread through the house causing their stomachs to rise up and confounding [their] brains. When the stench come I heard a great loud laugh from the boy (though I could not see him) and after the fit passed I could hear it still echoing for many minutes together.

Between the 3rd and 24th [of] March statements were took and the Mayor [of Carrickfergus] had arrested 8 persons as you well know: Janet Mean, of Braid Island; Jane Miller and Jane Latimer of Irish Quarter, Carrickfergus; Margaret Mitchell, of Kilroot (called by the others "Mrs. Ann" but found out by my description); Catherine M'Calmont, Janet

Liston (called Sellar), Elizabeth Sellar, and Janet Carson, all of Island Magee. [The women were brought up for trial on 31 March 1711, before Judges Upton (recipient of this letter) and James Macartney, both natives of County Antrim.] Those [the accused] swore to me privately that I should have no power to give evidence in court and indeed I did not know there where I was and could not speak being afflicted without mercy by three persons I never seen before, brought before me by the boy. These held me steady while he whispered me every manner of filth and lewdness.

The accused women had no lawyer, and the mental state of Mary Dunbar not being considered at that time a medical matter no such testimony was taken. All eight women strongly denied being witches, Jane Miller calling loudly for God to witness that she had been wronged. The court heard evidence concerning their characters, most of which was fairly damning, though this seems to have been more a result of their physical unattractiveness, the abrasiveness of their characters, their minority status (as Presbyterians), and the maliciousness these factors can give rise to in a small community, than of any particular information brought against them. As Seymour points out, most had recently taken communion, and several were evidently steady, industrious women; many were known to pray with their families both in private and in public, and most knew the Lord's Prayer, though it was generally said that since they were all Presbyterians they must have learned it in prison. (Witchcraft trials make some of the most sobering reading on earth.)

Judge Upton concluded his summation by saying that though he had no doubt the matter was diabolical in the genuine sense of that word, he also had no doubt that the jury should refuse to find the accused guilty on the basis merely of the visions of the afflicted woman. He concluded by saying that for himself he could not see how persons in compact with the Devil would be such "faithful attenders upon Divine Service." Judge Macartney, on the other hand, thought that the jury might very reasonably find them guilty. The jury agreed, and the eight women were sentenced to one year in jail, during which period they were to stand in the pillory four half-days. On these occasions the mob pelted them with the usual stones, rotten eggs, and vegetables, causing Janet Mean to lose an eye and Janet Carson to suffer a concussion and broken nose.

My tormentors being locked away [Mary Dunbar's letter concludes], Mr. Haltridge says I must get well and be lady to his wife. I thanked him on my knees, and he is a warm, handsome gentleman, sure. But last night The Boy come to me and would squeeze my arm until I cried out if I did not let him in my bed. There he makes himself a cat (though large for a cat), which the Devil has taught him—indeed, I'd wonder not were he the Devil himself—and these tricks and more he will teach me if I behave and do as he tells, for, says he, "We have work to do." "My mistress? says I." "No, says he, that bitch can wait." Truly he is a droll, comely lad at base and blessed with [super]natural powers.

And therefore out of your great kindness [of] which we have seen such evidence of late, tell me, good Sir (now it is Fools' Day), how a poor girl is to deny one who makes so large and energetic a cat? And tell me beside why you would call her before everybody a "poor visionary wretch?" And when you have considered these questions I expect you will want to attend one of these Divine Services of which you speak so high, and so you should, because you will need every Ally that you can muster in the Long Night that is a-coming for you. Sir, I am

Your most humble obedient servant,
Mary Dunbar

According to the Dictionary of Irish Biography, *Anthony Upton committed suicide on 11 September of the same year. The circumstances are not given. I been able to discover nothing about Mary Dunbar's subsequent career in the household of James Haltridge, but I do think that warm Mr. Haltridge had better have watched his step.*

---

[1]My principal sources, aside from Papers Relating to A. Upton, County Antrim (1703-11), British Museum Add. MSS. No. 31873, are St. John D. Seymour, *Irish Witchcraft and Demonology* (Dublin, 1913); Thomas Wright, *Narratives of Sorcery and Magic*, 2 vols. (London, 1851); Samuel MacSkimin, *The History and Antiquities of the County of the Town of Carrickfergus*, 2nd ed., ed. E.J. McCrum (Belfast, 1909); R.M. Young, *Historical Notices of Old Belfast and Its Vicinity* (Belfast, 1896); *Dublin University Magazine*, 82 (October 1873); *Hibernian Magazine*, 10 (January 1775).

IN THE SIXTIES

Four rooms, off-white and stipple, empty of furniture except a waterbed, a vanity, a scarred round table with a lamp. Two or three straight-backed chairs. Everything else was boxes of books and scattered items of Zochie's clothing, medicine, make-up, notes. The topic of furniture had never come up. When Nelson moved in he gave her a framed A.Y. Jackson print for the bedroom. She smashed it during their big first fight, after which she filled the wall it had hung on with anti-Nelson lipstick graffiti.

"Zochie, it's me! Don't you remember? I live here too!"

"I am sorry. I was sleeping."

Zochie unchained the door and kissed him. Sleep and smoke, old heat. Nelson hugged her, or tried to.

"Be careful of my cigarette!" she cried, brushing away ashes.

"Sorry. Can I open the drapes?"

"Drapes? It is Americans who say drapes."

"It is also Canadians who say drapes." He threw them open.

"Ooh, it's so bright," she said, searching for the hole.

"I'm sorry."

"I don't care about my clothes. You don't like this anyway. You haven't said one word about it. Don't you think it's nice?"

It was a tiger-skin print dressing gown, in silk.

"Sure."

"Screw you. Who cares. What I wear means nothing to me."

"You're beautiful anyway."

Zochie lit a cigarette, exhaled. "I know I'm beautiful," she said. "But I'm fucked up."

Nelson opened the balcony door. She had spent another day in bed. "That's right," he said. "You're more than a pretty face, you're insane."

"I was napping." The ashtray by the waterbed bloomed with crushed cigarettes, orange peels were scatttered around the sheets and floor, and a cord ran from the wall outlet to under the pillow. "That is not my problem. Won't you like some coffee?"

"No thanks." In the fridge he found margarine, an egg, cream cheese yellow along the edges, a bit of Gruyère, a withered eggplant, a saucer of crystalized anchovies. The egg he stirred with dry buckwheat in a hot skillet. When the grains were separate he poured in boiling water. The water went crazy on contact with the skillet. As the hissing and spitting died to boiling and the steam cloud started to move down the wall, he heard the vibrator from the bedroom. He clamped the lid on the skillet.

Zochie was propped against two pillows, one hand and the head of the machine between her legs. Nelson sat at her vanity and watched her face. She opened her eyes and smiled.

Nelson placed his ankle on his knee.

Zochie was moving her hips in a slow circle. She closed her eyes.

Nelson went to check the kasha. He stood on the balcony and looked down on rush-hour life. Moving right along. He wished every tree he saw could be in leaf. He wished he was under them, in green sunlight, green shadow. No, higher than the tip of the highest. Breathing sky. Breathing stars. The vibrator clicked off. Five more minutes for the kasha. He was hunting for butter when Zochie appeared at the kitchen door smoking a cigarette.

"I am so sexy because I am nervous about my examinations." She took a long drag. "Nelson, I am going to fail."

"That's my department."

"I am going to fail. It's not my intelligence, it's my English. You know how badly I write it, how slowly. I should have studied mathematics purely. I am going to fail. I will have to sleep with my professor. I will kill myself first. When will you fuck me? It doesn't matter. I am sore from the machine. I have used up orgasms for three days."

Zochie stood smoking and looking out over the city while Nelson ate.

"Have some kasha," he said.

Nelson slipped the key into the lobby door of the apartment building then walked back across the driveway to the oval of lawn in front, took off his shoes and socks, and dragged his feet through the dew, hands in his pockets, wanting Zochie to be home. He stretched out on the grass, dew soaking through his shirt.

"Nelson! What are you doing here? Nelson!" Zochie was kneeling to feel the grass. "It is too wet. You are drunk!"

He got up shivering. "Did you screw him?"

She was opening the door to the building with the key he had left in the lock. Swaying slightly. "Who?"

"Your professor."

"No. How could I go through with it. He is like potatoes."

"Did he try?"

"Yes. I was very nice to him. He thinks he will. That should be enough. He is so boring."

"Where'd you go?"

She shrugged. "The waiters sing there. His French is very bad."

They were riding the elevator.

"My French is bad too."

"Yes. But you are not like potatoes."

139

Nelson was shivering.

"You will have a cold sleeping on the grass."

While Zochie showered, Nelson stood in the darkened living room watching the lights of the city.

"Good night, Zochie!" he called when she went into the bedroom.

"Come in and kiss me goodnight."

He kissed her.

"Nelson, why don't you love me? Why do you despise me? I would like once to know."

Nelson looked at his watch. "Super says no fights after eleven."

Later he went out for a walk. When he got back, Zochie was gone. So was her toothbrush.

Towards noon the next day he collapsed on his way to shower. Nausea, mottled face in the mirror. Back to bed where he was when Zochie did not come home that night. Next morning he sat by the glass doors to the balcony in pale spring sunlight looking down on the street, eating toast and drinking tea.

And then he must have slept again. Zochie was in the bedroom, undressing to shower. "Hello my love. Did you have a nice time without me?"

"I caught flu."

"Oh, I'm sorry. Don't give it to me."

She disappeared into the bathroom. Emerging to dry herself, she said, "I am sorry you have caught flu."

Next morning he was standing on the balcony in his dressing gown when Zochie called goodbye. Goodbye. The sun was warm. He dressed and sat in it, spent most of the week like that, or in bed, while his body fought the sickness. Weeping as he watched the sun unfold delicate leaves the colour of lime Freshie, the rush hour traffic stall and honk down below, Zochie come in, shower, drink coffee, go out again.

When Nelson recovered he bought chickpeas, tahini, pita, a lemon. Four months after moving in he had found a blender under the sink, behind the garbage bucket. "Of course it works," Zochie had said. "I never use it because it makes too much noise. Cooking bores me."

"What are you doing?" she asked now.

"Making humous. Any paprika? It doesn't matter. How's the work?"

"Oh," lighting a cigarette, standing on one bare foot. "It's all right. I will pass."

"Perfect."

"No, not perfect. A miserable high second."

Nelson turned on the blender to cream the chickpeas, added more tahini. Zochie left and returned with a drink. Nelson was bent over watching creamed chickpea crawl towards the blades.

"What are you drinking?" he asked when he turned off the machine.

"Dubonnet. And I think I will have more."

"Go easy on me, Zochie, or I'll go out. Hey, there's lemon. There's ice." He made her a proper drink.

She picked the lemon slice off the rim and threw it into the sink. "Bourgeois shit."

When the humous was ready Nelson sprinkled cayenne on it to resemble paprika and carried it and a plate of hot pita into the living room. Zochie was hipshot at the window with an empty glass in her hand.

A knock at the door. With the plate on his knees, Nelson looked to Zochie, but she was on her way to the bedroom.

It was a woman named Dagmar. Nelson had met her at a party. She was standing in the hall radiating light in a six-inch aura. Nelson stepped back and she entered, removing gloves, shawls, wraps, scarves, embroidery-heavy Tibetan vest, motorcycle helmet. She passed the whole pile to Nelson.

"Watch my earrings," she said. "They're in the helmet."

Entering the living room, she said, "Oh. Are you just moving in?"

"Not really." As he passed down the hall to hang Dagmar's stuff in a closet, Zochie kicked shut the bedroom door.

"Is there someone else here?" Dagmar called from the living room.

"Yes."

"Oh. I thought you said you lived alone."

"I didn't think I said that."

Sound of breaking glass from the bedroom.

Zochie was half-dressed, holding a high heel. She had just smashed the mirror over her vanity. Her face was scarcely visible for cigarette smoke. Nelson moved warily, closing the door behind him. "What's the matter?"

"You were talking about me."

"Do you want her to leave?"

"No. I want to meet her. Why is she here?"

"To score. Please don't break anything else."

"No, my love."

"Zochie, she's absurd."

"Tell *her* this."

Nelson went back to the kitchen.

"What was it?" Dagmar called from the balcony.

"That was Zochie. She broke a mirror."

"On purpose?"

"She'll be out in a minute. Have some humous."

"Do you have anything to drink?"

"Water?"

"City water?" Dagmar asked, her eyes following Zochie

142

from the bedroom to the kitchen where a cupboard door opened. Zochie was pouring herself a drink.

"I think maybe there's some Dubonnet here," Nelson called to Dagmar. "Would you like some of that?"

"Dubonnet?" Dagmar asked.

Zochie appeared from the kitchen. "Dubonnet," she said, hand on her hip, raising her glass.

Nelson introduced them.

Zochie was wearing cream-coloured leather pants, a black silk top, high-heeled cork sandals.

The women smiled at each other.

"Could I try some?" Dagmar said.

"Of course," Zochie replied.

When Nelson placed the drink in her hand Dagmar smelled it. "It's alcoholic," she said.

Zochie looked at Nelson.

"Why, yes," he said. "I suppose Dubonnet is."

"I couldn't," Dagmar said, handing it back. "I can't meditate when I do, and I'm no good for anything when I don't meditate."

Zochie choked on her cigarette.

Dagmar scored a half ounce of Nepalese and had to rush away. At the door she turned, helmet in hand, and invited them both to dinner on Sunday. Nelson wrote down the address while Zochie stood deep in the room smoking. When the door closed Zochie went to the kitchen for a Dubonnet. A knock on the door. Dagmar was back for her earrings. She found them in her helmet and left again. Zochie sat at the table with her drink and a cigarette.

"That was Dagmar," Nelson said.

"Will you fuck her?"

"Only if you're there."

"I will not be."

"I'd rather you were. She makes me nervous."

"No. I have an exam on Monday. You go. I will stay here."

After a shower Nelson squeezed two oranges, added a little water and Vitamin C crystals, and sat with a glass of the results beside Zochie who moved only to light another cigarette.

"Nicotine kills vitamins," Nelson said at last, softly.

"Fuck off."

"I won't sleep with Dagmar. I prefer you."

"It is a choice? Do I prevent you?"

"No."

"So do it."

Zochie finished her drink on the way to the kitchen. She returned with a half inch of red wine, had emptied the Dubonnet. "You have no love for me," Zochie said.

"Christ."

"Nelson, it is *true!*"

"Then I should leave."

"*No!*"

"Zochie, they make flips this way."

"I am not a flip!" Zochie cried.

"I didn't say you were a flip."

"You said that you will be a flip if you stay here." She began to sob.

Nelson moved around the table, caught some wine in the face. "*Don't touch me!*" She ran to the bedroom and slammed the door. A few seconds later glass cracked. Nelson went to the balcony, to see a bullet-sized hole in the bedroom window. Her high heel again. Was she smashing her way out? He knocked on the door. The waterbed sloshed.

He returned to the living room and sat looking up at the stars. He got his winter coat from the closet and put it on over his pajamas and dressing gown and found a pair of stinking work socks in the clothes basket in the kitchen. Don't ask him why the kitchen. He put a pair of galoshes on over them and carried a chair onto the balcony where he sat in the spring night and watched for falling stars. An hour later he undressed in the hallway and crept into the bedroom. He undressed her—kissing her breasts—and climbed in beside her. The bed went heaving. She was snoring. He turned her onto her side and lay on his back, feeling the heat radiate from her back and legs down his side. He shut his eyes. Zochie was a soft bathtub, the engine of a melting car, a warm river. She moved. The raft rocked gently.

Dinner followed by a very strange, almost furtive hour on the floor and in bed with Dagmar, who declined an orgasm because her current lover was psychically attuned to her body, and Nelson was letting himself into the apartment building at midnight. He would shower. Zochie would be studying, have the door on the latch. She did. He knocked. She took a long time to come to the door and a long time to unfasten the latch. Avoiding his eyes, she returned to a fan of books and papers on the floor under a circle of light cast by the lamp, which sat on the very edge of the scarred round table.

"Hello," he said and noticed an empty mickey of gin on the table. "How's the work?"

"Could you pass me my cigarettes. Thanks. It is all right. I don't care about it. I have decided to go home. I hate this city."

Immediately the fear went thrilling up and down the backs of Nelson's legs. Three slow beats of his heart and it was into his throat. He swallowed. "Maybe you'll feel different after your exams."

"No." She exhaled. "I am going home."

"I don't want you to."

"No. You never loved me."

Her eyes were averted. Nelson went into the bedroom and closed the door. Methodically he undressed and got into bed. He lay on his stomach with the pillow over his head and cried. Got up, washed his face, and climbed back into bed. Lay on his back thinking how scared he was, until she crept in beside him, found his mouth with hers, all smoke and gin, and slipped him inside.

"Oh love," he said. "Oh love oh love oh love."

When his body was quiet she kissed his cheek. She went for a cigarette and smoked it lying with her back to him. When she finished the cigarette, she put the ashtray on the floor and turned towards him. He fell asleep, holding her in his arms, with the smell of her hair.

When he woke up the room was dark and Zochie was not there. He found her in the living room, leaned against the scarred little table, just outside the circle of light from the lamp. She was sitting on one foot, with the tiger-skin gown loose around her shoulders, her head bowed as if she were studying the hand that lay palm upwards in her lap.

"Zochie, what are you doing? Come to bed."

Her head swung up and she looked at him as if trying to remember who he was. Suddenly she laughed. The arm that was not in her lap lay heavy on the table. She tried to swing it clear of the lamp to salute him with her glass, but she clipped the lampshade and the lamp teetered. The circle of light shifted and the shadows went swaying. "What am I doing?" she said. "What is Zochie doing? She is asking herself why her love does not love her. Why this boy who is too simple to be bad treats her like a whore."

"Oh shit, Zochie, please! Come to bed. You're drunk."

"Yes, I am drunk."

"Will you come to bed?"

She laughed. "Didn't you know, my love? Whores never sleep at night."

146

Nelson returned to bed thinking how theatrical she was, how difficult; thinking what a relief to be free from that inexorable mind. But he could not stop being afraid. Suddenly he gave a start and was wide awake—like Zochie herself often, or like a child—with a night terror, but there was nothing, no vision, only the continuing darkness and the crack of light under the door. And then there was something there, something small and potent, blossoming.

He found her in the living room curled in the circle of light with her knees up and her arms against her breasts. At first he thought the darkness by her head was a shadow cast by the lamp, but it was not. She was cuddled into what might have been a pool of blood if her notes and dressing gown had not been under to soak it up. He held the lamp to her face. He rummaged through the kitchen drawer for clean dish towels. He wrapped her wrists. He found an empty bottle of barbituates but could not tell how many she had taken. He phoned a cab—an ambulance would have meant it was too serious—and was still fussing with dressing her when the buzzer sounded.

In the cab she came to consciousness begging him please not to blame her, not to be mad, to forgive her, not to let them take her to the hospital. He told her they were going to the hospital because she had swallowed pills.

"Not too many. Only to forget. Don't be angry. Please forgive me. I love you so much."

Nelson shut his eyes.

An orderly was sitting in a wheelchair just inside the Emergency doors. He got up and beckoned Zochie into the seat as if she had come in for a haircut. The smell of hospital was suffocating. For Nelson it was frightening and reassuring but reassuring in a way that was also frightening. The orderly wheeled Zochie down a broad corridor. A nurse appeared from a doorway, glanced at Zochie, and said something to the orderly. Nelson started towards her but was called back by another nurse, who asked for Zochie's date of birth, name, address, what she had swallowed, how much approximately, and how long she had been drinking. The other nurse reached for the information sheet. Nelson was told to sit down.

He crossed and uncrossed his legs in a moulded plastic chair across from a very pale old man asleep in his coat with his hat on his lap. He shuffled magazines on an arborite table without thinking. He got up to walk around, afraid the reception nurse would order him back to his seat. The sounds that he, and he alone, it seemed, was hearing from down the corridor were Zochie's gagging, wailed objections to having her stomach pumped. A nurse was shouting at her. The gagging, objections, and reprimands went on for a long time. Periodically the nurse gave an instruction to someone else. Twenty minutes after all noise had suddenly ended, the orderly returned with the wheelchair and told Nelson he would find her through the third door on the left.

Zochie was at the near end of an apparently uninhabited, shadowy room filled with beds half obscured by white curtains. She was strapped onto a high narrow bed with wheels. The clothes he had dressed her in were jumbled underneath in a metal lattice like a shopping basket. She was wearing a hospital nightgown in two shades of faded blue check, tied at the back. A white sheet, drawn under her arms, was spattered with vomit. Her wrists had been bandaged.

"Come to see me tomorrow," she said. She was very pale, her eyes hardly open at all.

"Sure."

"I'm sorry."

"It's OK."

"Don't despise me."

"I don't despise you."

"I am ashamed."

"It doesn't matter."

"They will try to commit me."

"No they won't."

"They will deport me."

"No."

"Come to see me tomorrow."

Back at Zochie's, Nelson scrubbed the kitchen sink and filled it with cold water to soak her tiger-skin dressing gown. He wiped blood off her notes in the bathroom sink and spread them flat on newspaper in the living room. He opened the curtains and got into bed as the sun paused on the horizon a moment to perfect itself before lifting off.

WATCHES

On New Year's Eve it will be four years since I had my first and only conversation with a watchmaker, a Mr. Tigman, Kristine's father. Kristine is the wife of my old friend Dan, who was working that night (of all nights) with a computer downtown. Kristine had nothing planned, except possibly a few hours at a Swiss New Year's party, which for some reason did not begin until one in the morning. I was supposed to meet some friends who had promised to welcome the New Year at my apartment, but at the last minute they had changed their minds, and I, like Kristine, was left with nothing to do between seven and one on New Year's Eve.

For three or four years in my late twenties I succeeded in living so far removed from the world that annual milestones meant nothing to me. New Year's Eve was no different from any other eve. But once a person re-enters the world he accepts the burden, because he accepts the anticipation, of such occasions, and not to be able to enjoy the prospect of having a good time on New Year's Eve can be very depressing. So I phoned Kristine, who was staying at her parents', and we arranged, awkwardly, because I still love her, to drive downtown for a drink and dinner. Laughing, Kristine said that my company would be a perfect compromise between doing nothing and doing something she did not want to do at all.

When I arrived, her little girl Hilary was still up, being a giraffe, nibbling the coleus; her mother was fussing with the dog, who had a temperature; and her father sat with the paper in a small, brightly lit living room. I was offered a seat across from him while Kristine put her over-excited child to bed. I am no good socially, but for the first ten or fifteen minutes in the company of someone I have just met, I can manage a creditable though stiff sort of conversation. Aware that Kristine's father had been a watchmaker, I asked him if he knew that Uri Geller was now living secluded with his family in a German forest, and that his child apppears to have the same abilities. When Mr. Tigman asked who Uri Geller was, I told my story about having once met him at a party, where with my own eyes I saw him make a watch I personally knew to be broken start going again, simply by staring at it. It is not possible, Mr. Tigman said quickly. You have been deceived. This Geller is a magician of some sort. I nodded reflectively, then mentioned that my brother has never been able to wear a watch, and neither could our grandmother. Did Mr. Tigman think it might have something to do with electricity? The body's magnetic field? Should my brother take up dowsing? Their watches are faulty, Mr. Tigman replied. In thirty-seven years of repairing watches in Zurich and Montreal (he had retired a few months earlier) he had never known one that was not flawed or dirty not to run as it should. I told him that up north one morning I awoke with my space heater gone out and the temperature in my cabin at minus thirty-nine degrees; in fact, it was so cold that my quartz watch, on the bedtable beside me, had stopped. He shrugged. It was not possible. The cold must have affected your senses.

We talked for a while about digital watches. I exaggerated my amazement that manufacturers could switch the reading of time from the right brain to the left and nobody even notice. I argued that digital time is lots more insistent, more undeniable, makes the passage of the damn stuff more concrete, objective, inexorable, and a whole lot less imaginable. I complained about this. Mr. Tigman had no use for digital watches. No, he was not trained to repair them. He laughed at the absurdity of paying so much for a watch and then

151

having to press a button to see the time. I reminded him they were not all like that. He said that people take them back within a few months because they have worn out the batteries showing their new toy to friends. I said that nowadays it seemed the less you paid the better watch you got— if you did not mind a plastic strap. He made no reply. After a silence I told him that the watch I happened to be wearing, a self-winding Timex, stopped every night at 11:25, even if I jiggled it and wound it by hand at 11:20. Why? Dirt, he said. Should I have it cleaned? In the case of a Timex, he replied, you would be more sensible to take a hammer to it. When he saw that he had shocked me he added, more kindly, Buy a new one.

Kristine returned to the living room. She was still an artist at that time, a painter of landscapes, up and down the Ottawa Valley, but she was not happy, because of what—as she put it later that night—working for Xerox was doing to her husband's balls. Her latest ambition was to become a lawyer in order to support the family while he went back to writing novels. She came into the room carrying a book of sample questions for the law school entrance exams. She sat down and answered my thin, informal questions about the exams and about the book, fanning the pages nervously, all her real attention focussed not upon me or upon her father's silence but upon the sputtering fuse of some old keg of violence inside herself. As I tried to elicit her reasons for wanting to give up the creative life, I knew that I was after some kind of detonation to blow away the scientistic old bastard. She said first in an embarrassed, rehearsed way that community legal work had always interested her, that she had always wanted to help people with concrete problems. Anyway, she said, the visual arts are bankrupt. She said she was fed up with struggling to create works of art that people buy to decorate their homes. She then paused as if considering how to express what it is like to be an artist for philistines, when suddenly her father delivered one of those ritual parental blows to the heart that leave children, of whatever age, amazed and staggering. And for the first time in your life, he said, you will earn steady money. Radiant with animus, Kristine walked out of the room. As for me, how could I help it? Carefully I laid my Timex on the little strip of marble that passed for a hearth in that bright little room. Isn't this what you wanted? I asked the old man with a laugh, and smashed it with a poker.

As we drove downtown, me trembling with excitement, Kristine told me that all her life her father had been telling her she had to earn her own living. In high school she had done well in maths and physics, but at university she went into Fine Art to spite him. I told her about Uri Geller and my brother's inability to wear watches. He's such a narrow bastard, she said. He's got his little house, his TV, his freezer, and his car. He's got everything he ever wanted, and he expects everybody to do the same thing. All they ever talk about is how constipated the dog is or what's on TV. Speaking of TV, I interjected, did you see Uri Geller bend those forks the other night? I wanted to pull over and touch her. Her anger made her complete within herself, like a doll or an erotic picture. I did not, of course. We had dinner, the only couple in the restaurant. Like an ass, I proposed a toast to the Law. At midnight the waiters blew horns. When I took her home her parents' house was dark. We sat in the driveway. Neither of us knew what to say. She had developed a headache during the meal. I am not easy company. I told her that Andy Warhol once said he likes going to Switzerland because nothing ever happens there. She asked me what time it was. One twenty-five, I guessed. Only clockwork cuckoos coming out of strong-hinged little doors. I wanted to kiss her. She thanked me for everything and got out of the car.

* * *

153

My stepmother had social pretensions. She gave up many of them when she married my father, but still I was sent away to an exclusive boarding school near Montreal, where I did not fit in. My father had been earning good money renovating houses—he could afford the school—but my upbringing had not been that of a professional man's son. My schoolmates were aliens to me: quick, sophisticated, inflexible, brutal. I was miserable there. I had been gone two terms when my father died. I remember going home for his funeral, sitting on the train watching great thunderheads move across the sun and thinking that the silver lining for me was that I would not have to go back to that awful school. I was wrong. A week later I was back in my old seat, stupid with misery. Wearing my father's watch.

But there was one good thing about that school: Mr. Lachine, the science master. He would arrive back from his parents' farm on Monday morning and pace the classroom telling us, with his earnest bumpkin face, while we hooted and scoffed, about his fear of being irradiated by their TV set. I was no country boy, but at that school I felt as out of place as he was, and saw him as a kindred spirit. For a master he was unusual because of being so kind and personal with the boys, and not in any neurotic or sexual way. He crumpled an oil tin for us by pumping the air out of it, and he made a banana-flavoured drink from four vials of colourless, tasteless liquid. Another time he brought in a geiger counter and let the class put their watches under it. I hung back, afraid that my father's watch was too cheap for that company. The phosphorescent stuff that made it glow in the dark had been daubed around the dial carelessly, it seemed to me. When Mr. Lachine noticed me at the rear of the group he made me step forward and stretch out my arm. Immediately the sinister ratchet sound became loud and frantic. The needle went crazy. Everybody shouted with laughter. I was frightened and embarrassed, but also proud to have such a potent, unusual watch. For the last day of classes Mr. Lachine prepared short comic biographies for each of us when we were forty, and read them out. I was lately deceased, from radioactive poisoning.

* * *

I remember one afternoon when I was four or five asking the girl digging alongside me in a sandbank for the time. She stared at her bare wrist and said, Two hairs past a mole a quarter to a freckle, and then looked at me. I did not know what to do. In fact, I knew perfectly well what time it was. I had chosen the question for sounding gruff and perfunctory and for not sounding as though I was trying to get her to talk to me. I had also chosen it because I knew the answer, and I felt that would give me the upper hand. You may recognize first love in this. My only apology for a stratagem is that I developed it myself, with my own cunning. My defences were as Innocent as my love, whereas her answer was a cold wind from the wastes of Experience, and it levelled everything.

Why? Because *Two hairs past a mole a quarter to a freckle* was not hers. She had picked it up from some context foreign to both of us and was using it unexamined, just as an adult will use unexamined the queer lifeless language of conventional opinion. There was also, I suppose, my sense of being found out. She had non-answered my non-question. And yet in doing so had splashed herself with the muck of vulgar particularity, of hairs and freckles and moles. And then there was this other element, this willingness not only to tell somebody else's joke, not only to mock my stratagem, not only to smirch my love with physicality—self-conscious physicality at that—but to pretend that her body could do for a machine, a thing that ticks . . . I hit her across the side of the head with my shovel. She put her hand to her ear and got to her feet in silence. She walked away slowly. I heard her gulp for air, and then she started to run.

* * *

Many habits nobody understands but few nobody talks about at all. Some are not talked about because they are invisible, assimilated without seams into the fabric of personality, or large as lifetimes: too big to be seen. Others are small, like tics. They catch the eye and are understood or not, as the case may be. Still others are obvious but ignored, probably because they appear to link us to animals or machines in unfashionable ways. Ignored, they go unseen.

For example. At this moment I am sitting on the third floor of the Toronto Public Library on Yonge Street. The man across the table from me is looking up items in the *Guinness Book of Records*. Occasionally he refers to a sheaf of papers on his left. He is making notes in a neat hand on 6 x 4 filecards. As he works, he smells his left wrist. This is how he does it. Between his top teeth and bottom lip he takes a fold of skin from the upper side of his wrist and lets go, breathing through his mouth on the place, then smelling it. He does this repeatedly, the smelling usually either following a series of bites or following each bite in a leisurely way. Sometimes there is no bite at all, simply an exhalation through the mouth followed immediately by an inhalation through the nose. When there is no bite I can still tell what he is doing by the rotation of his wrist as he shifts the breathed-on spot back under his nose.

The nose is a penis, Freud tells us, and the thumb is a breast; we pick when we would masturbate and suck when we would suckle. So what is the wrist? And what is all this sniffing that goes on? Nothing, because it has not yet been acknowledged. One of the most common human habits, as

156

common as nose-picking and not half as offensive, and nobody talks about it. This man across the table from me in the Toronto Public Library has been smelling his wrist in full public view for an hour, and no one bats an eye.

I used to have a theory I developed watching people study in the stacks at university. If you watch them you see how busy they are with their hands and feet. They fiddle and jiggle, they stroke their faces, they twist their hair, they smell their wrists. My theory explained all this activity as the outcome of one's need when moving in abstract realms to keep on reminding oneself of the body, lest one float away, as it were. When I saw the absurdity of the mind/body division, I stopped believing this theory. Now it seems to me that thought is a physical process, a particular sort of activity the mind can engage in locally in the brain, but one that constitutes a fragmentation of mental energy, that sends it scattering off to generate other, more visible habits and tics. I do believe this, but with regard to wrist-smelling it does not quite seem adequate. Now when I think of wrist-smelling a jumble of things comes to mind: our olfactory impoverishment, our air at once deodorized and polluted; women wearing perfumes to mask their womanly odours (dabbing it where? on their wrists, of course, where the skin is "thin," and behind their ears); Arabs, out of politeness, standing close enough to allow you whiffs of their breath; smokers, made addicts by the nicotine and sugar in cigarettes, by the need to fit in, to relax, to do something with their hands, but also surely by the need to taste with the lungs; dogs living their lives through their noses, up and down the rollercoaster pathways of scent; penis noses penetrating the auras of vulva wrists; the man who has eaten human flesh telling you with a foolish grin that it tastes just like chicken; the universal male custom of smelling girls' bicycle seats; the Chinese, with their utterly alien sanity, their incense clocks measuring time by shifts of scent; myself as a boy not able to feel the pain until after the fight, as a man not able to smell a woman again until we have finished making love; children pressing security blankets under their noses; a fetishist enthusing to me about the thrill of the smell of leather, and when I asked him about the factor of domination, the tantalizing, vulnerable purity of pale skin inside black leather, affronted; my father, a Rosicrucian, sitting on the edge of his bed last thing at night, holding a glass of warm water to his lips, closing the circuit of his energy.

Finally, my watch, my *wrist*watch. Its strap is calfskin. The calfskin has a musky smell part mine and part the calf's, and if I scratch my nail along the inside of it I have a dirty nail. I like to think my watchstrap has soaked up me. On the third floor of the Toronto Public Library I place my watch on the table to the left of my papers. I write a bit, look around, watch the man across from me sniff his wrist, and write again. A trace of the disinfectant smell of soap remains on my wrist from my shower this morning. I find it unpleasant. I smell my watchstrap instead. The man across the table and I are both at it, sniffing and sniffing . . . It occurs to me, and I have just barked with laughter and got more stares than my wrist-smelling friend will ever get, that if I am ever starving to death I intend to *eat my watch.*

* * *

Back to Uri Geller, who, by the way, keeps himself in pocket these days locating ore for international mining companies and enemy warhead placements for the Americans. My parents separated when I was four; when I was seven my father married the woman who sent me to the boarding school near Montreal. My real mother disappeared from my life until one Easter, when she visited me in the company of her daughter by her third husband. From the moment I saw her, this girl, my mother's daughter, exerted an unholy hold on me. She must have been aware of it, not because at fifteen she lacked innocence, but because my solicitude tends to paw. I looked at her face and saw mine, if mine were young and innocent and beautiful. Of course she was too young, less than half my age. My intimate manner with her was avuncular and strained, real Humbert Humbert stuff, it dated and shamed me. Each generation has its own structure of feeling. I was willing to do anything to get that girl to talk to me, but it was hard, so hard, to find common ground. When I told her about Uri Geller she listened as if she were simple or I were mad. When I finished I thought she must be thinking of some graceful way to excuse herself, and then she told me, in a voice I had to strain to hear, that after watching Uri Geller on TV she had taken a broken watch from her mother's drawer and made it go by looking at it. She held her wrist towards me. It's still going, she said.

By God, it was.

I was boisterous with admiration. I kissed her hand. I scrutinized her watch like a pawnbroker. She pulled back. I saw my error. More calmly, to draw her out, I asked, Was she standing in front of the TV when it happened? Was she certain the watch was broken? Did she wind it as she took it from the drawer? She looked away and said nothing, her fingers twisting in her lap. I backed off, leaving her to silence, conscious of being violently irritated by her, the way an adolescent will be irritated, will be motivated to vandalism, by dumb nature. I also found myself wondering if her shyness was not a simple effect of her lying to me about starting the watch.

And then last week I had dinner with my old friends Dan and Kristine. While Kristine was in the kitchen putting dessert together, Dan asked me if I had noticed the spoons, and I realized when he said this that they had been jiggling all through the meal, as if a distant train had never stopped passing. He told me that when they first bought their dining room table—a thick, grey-tinted slab of glass supported by two pieces of curving tubular metal—it was absolutely solid. Since the bolts were all screwed tight and the floor it stood on was thickly carpeted, it ought to have been. But in the last six months it had begun to vibrate. Well, I said, what in the house has changed in the past six months? Nothing, said Dan, pouring me another glass of wine. It must be the traffic, he said. How old is Hilary? I asked. The last time I saw her she was being an excellent giraffe. He assumed I had changed the subject. Thirteen, he said. She's quite the lady now. Maybe it's a poltergeist, I said. When I finally got Dan to hear this he dismissed it. To my annoyance. When Kristine came back I repeated it to her. Kristine was scarcely happier with the idea than Dan but agreed it was possible. Thereby she confirmed his old suspicion that I encourage her in all manner of occult folly.

In the days when Dan I knew each other better than either of us knew Kristine, and when all our bodies were beautiful, the three of us rented a cottage on Georgian Bay for a week and spent most of the time in bed. One afternoon, taking a breather, we played telepathy games and found a pattern emerging. Kristine was picking up approximately one in three of my mental images. On the theory that emotion is a violent disturbance in the brain, and that disturbance is more readily transmittable than quietness, I was concentrating on images that aroused emotion in me, for example, that watch of my father's with the fluorescent paint slopped around the dial. What Kristine picked up, with no clues whatsoever and never having heard the story about my watch and the school geiger counter, was circles of glowing things behind glass. That was close enough for me, but Dan, feeling, I suppose, left out, and with the crankiness of the bored libertine, became obstinate. He argued that the mind is capable of abstracting an infinite number of details from any image but chooses only two or three, the two or three it needs, and having done so is rarely capable of imagining more than a few alternatives, whereas the number of possible alternatives can be enormous. He asked me to consider seriously how many other impressions—besides circles glowing behind glass—I would accept to signify my watch. My reply was the kind that truly dumbfounds the logical. I am too ashamed to remember it exactly now; it was the equivalent of: That is all very well as theory, Dan, but in this case it is clear that the facts indicate otherwise. I know Dan was offended; I could see it in his eyes. I knew he believed that I was being willful and false in order to assert a belief in Kristine and the irrational that he could never share, and I returned his gaze defiantly.

At dinner the other night the subject turned from poltergeists to my favourite bugbear Uri Geller. Dan said he had seen TV magicans do the same things by trickery. Being professionals they never, of course, explain how they do it, but sleight of hand and traditional techniques were more likely explanations than supernatural powers. My point, in reply, was that magicians who appear on network TV are necessarily professional media people, who know that it is easier to catch the public's attention by exposing Geller as a fraud than by jumping on his bandwagon. It is as likely, I argued, that they have powers similar to Geller's as that they have so-called traditional ways of doing the same extraordinary things. Without looking at me, and raising his voice slightly, Dan described a few more ostensibly inexplicable tricks he had seen performed by self-proclaimed frauds. In other words, he refused to acknowledge my point. Of course he is older than he once was, and between the three of us we had drunk three bottles of wine on top of cocktails. Kristine, who seemed tired, refused to join in; several times she tried to change the subject. When Dan stopped talking he emptied his glass. He must have been drunk. For several seconds he sat with his head thrown back. Silently I counted to five, then, stripping my voice of all earnestness, as if refusing out of disdain for the state of the conversation to commit myself to the truth of what I was saying, I reported that my fifteen-year-old stepsister had once made a watch go after seeing Uri Geller on TV. Instead of responding, Dan stood up and suggested we move into the living room. Immediately I was on my feet, causing the spoons fresh jiggling, drunk yes, but groping around inside for the key to the emotion this galvanic tractability was supposed to hide.

I followed Dan into the living room. There like a little boy he began to show me his new digital watch. Kristine came in and said it was silly because now when she asked him the time he said 8:02 instead of eight o'clock, and it was like being in the army. Bullshit, Dan replied. In the army you would say twenty hundred hours. Kristine, somewhat defeated these days by Dan, I think, and by the awful life of a housewife, went to bed. Dan must have assumed her distrust of technology was also something she had got from me, because he insisted I tell him what I really thought about his new watch. After some coyness I said I liked the way it went *beep beep* on the hour, and wasn't that awkward at concerts. I said it reminded me of a TV screen. I said all kinds of stupid things. I said I loved those watches you could see the workings of, because they looked like a joke, portholes into the wrist. I said the only good thing about time is the white shadows that watches leave on the wrists of golden women. White breasts, white buttocks, white time scars, but wasn't it true that a woman is more likely to leave a digital watch on, and that's sexy too? A mean-looking watch can do wonders for a naked woman? I said I like expansion bands because they catch the hairs, little tugs of mortality. I said that time ought to be human. It needs a circle, the sweep of hands. This flashing of

162

numerals has no heart, it's outer space stuff, flash flash flash to goddam infinity. I think I must have been shouting. I was as drunk as Dan, and I know he was shouting. I remember him stretched out in a chair with his face in his hands, talking at the same time I was, telling me what a bizarre thing it was that I was the only real friend he had, calling me a crank and a phony and a hell of a horny weird bastard. Later, at the door, as he was telling me in the most horribly maudlin way how much he loved Kristine— this woman you have destroyed, I wanted to say—I realized their daughter Hilary was sitting at the top of the stairs in a night dress, hugging her knees. How long had she been there, listening to everything? I looked at my watch, expecting to see the hands crimped and doubled like bobby pins. And then on the doorstep, to my embarrassment, Dan embraced me, for a long time. He was crying. I could hardly stand it. I thought of tearing off his stupid new watch and throwing it away, imagined it climbing the night sky, the facets of the vulgar expansion band lit by blue fluorescence from the street lamps. A satellite, with many angled panels, an instrument for talking to stars. As he swore to have me over again soon, to love me better, and all kinds of other morbid nonsense, I broke away. "Daddy!" I heard Hilary cry. The door closed. While the screen door, one of those pneumatic, aluminum ones, was still making passes at closing, I began to crawl down the lawn. Before I reached the sidewalk and, beyond it, presumably, my car, I decided to take a nap, a ten-minute nap. When I say ten minutes, I mean ten minutes. I am convinced that anyone who naps can nap to the second. Never mind how long things may seem, the best clock is the clock in the head. I looked at my watch, a quartz Pulsar with a sweep hand: 1:32:10,11,12. I thought about 1:42:10,11,12. I closed my eyes. I opened them. *1:42:11.*

Exactly. I continued my journey.

SECRET WAR

Woke up in 1959 month of September mailbox key gone. Spoke to postmaster who said No replacement. Girl in post office opened it for me, boss gone to lunch, my insurance book cheques all my mail come out burned in half. Three days later we left for Calgary trailed by two women who got on when we did. Three different times in lounge car they tried to start fights with my mother who turned away twice, third time threw beer in their face. She was robbed on that train outside Sudbury cold grey morning no help from the porter, a Newfie or so he claimed. Got to Wilcox Hotel Winnipeg for almost two weeks stalked day and night by same two women. No hot in the room, head-size holes punched in all four walls, a wrench no use on the rads. Got a phone call: Come home. Stepfather died, reason for death don't know, something strange killed him as we were told. Six months later mother died reason for death heart blockage. Hold on Momma, I says, too late.

1962 Windsor Ontario attacked by factory mob led by police informant I was fined. Not enough space to put down all trouble over next ten years. 1972 my car towed from garage where muffler was blown and I get billed $27 a day for storage wouldn't tell me where car was. Had to go to Toronto and when they come to my case I was told to get the RCMP, which I did. But no car. Left Windsor 1972 the month of November into Port Credit working for a Carl Evans Jr. warehouse job, RCMP still come around. Gave them my story in a phone booth there was nothing that they would do. Whole shipments missing then, the inventory man gone two weeks, all suspicion directly on me. Put on jacket and tie to see Mr. Evans, the boys tip tar over the ledge of the roof I walk in tar all over me upset the whole office. Evans takes carpet cleaning out of my termination.

Living in Timmins then two weeks the flood hits my door, lifts my trailer 200 yards and folds it around a rock. Call my insurance man who tells me, Sorry no clause for floods, and I thought he said cause. *Spring run-off!* I shout but he hung up. I move on to Kirkland new trailer. My neighbour tells me the OPP kicked down my door looking for concealed weapons. I call them up and they say I am parked illegal on the pole. Not that I knew. No fine ever came. But back at my trailer someone cut through my outside thin plate and come out in my closet. The open door was them leaving with my TV fridge stereo broke my earphones in two. Nobody ever seen them. There was no insurance to phone. I stayed there three weeks on the pole, no work. They cut me off then and I stayed two-three more days, could not get out of bed not even for stickiness. A cop brought a summons and I walked out past him to the highway, hitched back south or tried. One car stopped, backed over my suitcase, drove off. An OPP searched me on shoulder near Gravenhurst and I got his name. Was told he didn't exist. That makes two of us I told them. In Barrie met a married woman who went to school with him. I showed her the guns. Got a trailer site near Ajax signed on Thursday, Friday the man said he didn't want me in his park. I got some legal defense help and the last thing the girl said was, Mister, you got some high dark corners in your head watch out.

Watch out indeed. I was in that trailer park two weeks when a woman says they have gone in the office against me. My back door is ruined see for yourself. Was a good door, double thickness. Since I move in all I hear is they want me out. Food stamps stolen drying on my steps I phone up they want me in court signing papers. Got a job on the pumps had my wallet stolen by a kid in the backseat, isn't he cute? his mother ask me. No, lady, the boy is a thief. They broke in and cleared out the till the suspicion falling clean on me, an old pattern. The boss says he accepts my word but I know now he took it himself. There is not enough paper to put down all the evil that has been done in the name of the truth and other fine laws. As wise old Churchill once said, "Secret war is the name of the game." I sit here in this office electric heater not working for two days fingers stiff thinking over these things left with one clear choice. There is Highway 401 and there is the time in his own defense a man will say OK everybody that's enough, stop, turn, walk in some place, and open fire.

KINGBIRD

It was her normal voice, but William was falling towards sleep and it jolted him.

"Wha—" he said.

Susan Kingbird was leaning against the headboard, an arm across her stomach, smoking a cigarette. "I said, Why not move in here."

William lived next door.

Why not indeed. Of course, put him on a high cliff and he would throw himself over.

"Rent out yours," she said. "Then I won't have to see Cates."

See. "I thought you were finished with Cates."

"I am, but you know."

Everything he could think of to say next sounded too critical. He kept quiet and then he said, "What if your husband comes back?"

"*Carl*? What if we all die tomorrow."

Later William remembered a car in the night.

At seven he was up for work, a half Saturday. On her front step was a jar of what looked like apple juice, but the label said FIRE WATER and had been put together from newspaper headlines.

William poured it down the drain. He tore off the label and buried the jar in the garbage can under the sink.

When he was back in his own house that afternoon he called Cates.

"Billy Duzak!" Cates cried. "What? OK. How about right now. Always available."

Two hours later Cates was squeezing out of his big

Oldsmobile and William was at his screen door drying his hands on a dish towel. Cates shouted at him to open two beers.

Cates could not fit into either of William's lawnchairs, so he squatted with his back against the trunk of a willow tree that was technically on Kingbird's property but that had long ago consumed a wire fence of William's and later burst through a picket one. He undid his pants.

"It's hot, eh?" Cates said. "Robust types like me take a beating in this weather. Not like you rail-skinny Polack sons of bitches."

Cates kicked off his white loafers. His socks were banana-yellow, like nylons around the toes. "Let's have another one," he said.

When William came back with the beer, a small black beetle had dropped from the willow to crawl around on Cates' shoulder.

"It's a nice little place you've got out here, William. A man could go Indian just for the quiet. One day—you can quote me—you're going to see sewers out here. I'm on your side, William. Every step of the way. Listen to the little people. That's how you survive a quarter century in politics. What can I do for you."

"No more piss on her doorstep," William said.

Cates had a fat man's complaisance of expression, and it did not visibly alter now, except around the eyes. With difficulty Cates rose to his feet. He sucked in his stomach, legs stiff, and pulled up his fly.

"I don't know what you're talking about," he said.

At his car Cates paused a moment with both hands on the door and his head down while William stared at the ridge of bone along the back of the cropped head. And then Cates got in and started the engine. William stepped into the man's vacated pose, straight-armed against the door, feeling the top of the window across his fingers, watching the beetle try to find its way down off the edge of Cates' collar.

"Insult her again," William said, "and I'll come and find you myself."

Cates was looking straight ahead. "Duzak. If now you're telling me you think you're the champion of that clapped-out whore, then I would say it's time to move back to town."

Cates slapped at his neck. He took his foot off the brake and backed, spinning tires, down William's lane. On the concession road, as if once more in the public realm, he pulled away with stately acceleration.

William was walking over to pick up Cates' beer cans when, for the first time in two years, he saw the old Ford Fairlane, pulled right up to her front step. At that same moment her door flew open and Susan called, "Hey, William! Come on over and say hi to Carl!"

William had no time to refuse before she disappeared back inside.

When he came into the kitchen she said, "You know Carl."

Carl Kingbird nodded but did not get up; he indicated a chair. William sat down, accepted a cup of coffee from Susan. Kingbird was a six-and-a-half foot Cree with a bad complexion. In his lap he held a brindle cat. Very slowly, without smiling, he leaned forward and extended his hand. William shook it.

"She told me," Kingbird said, "your wife died. I was sorry to hear that."

William nodded. "A year ago," he said.

Kingbird looked at Susan, who got up and poured him more coffee. "I was more than two years dead for my wife," Kingbird said. "That's over now."

William looked to Susan. She dropped her eyes, crossed to the sink. When she turned on the taps the water pipes hammered. Kingbird looked around at her without annoyance and back at William, who finished his coffee.

"You and me, eh Duzak," Kingbird said. "Neighbours again."

"That's right."

"Anything we should talk about now that I'm back?"

"Nothing comes to mind at this minute," William said. He stood up. "But I'll be in touch as soon as that willow gets to my septic tank."

Kingbird smiled. He was leaning slightly forward with his enormous hands spread on his knees, almost as if he were contemplating seeing William to the door. "With men like Cates in power," Kingbird said, "the whole world'll have sewers before then."

Later that afternoon it was hotter still, and there was no breeze. William was down on his knees, weeding his lawn, when Susan came over to the fence.

"He's staying?" William said after a silence.

"Says he is."

William did not reply.

"God, it's great having him back," Susan said.

"Two years."

She laughed. "*Over* two years, William! I must be crazy!"

Later Carl Kingbird came out of the house and stood gazing up at the willow. When he saw William he did a chainsaw pantomime and laughed. After a few minutes Susan came out, and Kingbird stood talking to her. William shut his eyes; he could feel the force of the sun on his face. When William opened his eyes, Kingbird and Susan, in the heat and the stirred dust of the driveway, in the silence, were dancing.

THE FALLING NIGHT

You are coming down out of the north for the first time in three months. The city is a day's drive, half of it down this corridor of jack pines and whipping telephone poles. The sun is liquid, crimson, it is giant, and it hangs for a moment reflected in a vast, black-ice beaver swamp. Against the red ball of it stands a hydro tower in precise silhouette. The windshield is clean, there are no insects yet, and you can see every wire strung on that tower.

Suddenly you must swerve to miss a pile of fur. You pull over, walk back, and drag a young Labrador to the shoulder. Some kid has lost his dog. For a few seconds you stare at the smashed thing—it is no more than a sack of blood and bones—and you wonder how there can be any connection between this and something alive. Such wreckage happens to people too, all the time, on highways just like this, and you wonder what love is supposed to mean among such destructable beings. Somebody once said that to be in love with a person is to overestimate the details that distinguish that person from others. And now you wonder if love is some kind of hysterical refusal of this terrible, final sameness.

As you get back into your car your eyes fall on a slat of wood, nailed to a tree. There is a lane, and on the slat an uneven row of metallic squares framing black letters: HACKETT. You drive in to ask the Hacketts if they own a Lab pup, but the person who answers the door, a startled woman with a moustached, rubbery mouth, says, "*What?*" and from a back room a querulous voice shouts that you had better not try any funny business, because he knows your game. The woman glares with her mouth set in defiance. You say, "I don't understand," and turn away. But you do understand.

Night is falling, and you are driving too fast. The water in the ditches will have road salt in it; there could be moose out, hungry for sodium. Still you do not slow down. Later, when it gets dark. By then you will be down off this rock into farmland, where cruisers with radar wait on the shoulder. You reach for the tape deck, but your tapes have been boring you for a long time. From the radio you get blasts of staticky noise that sounds as if it is being transmitted from the underbelly of a prop-engine bomber. You turn it off.

Here and there the solitary golden windows blink through the trees. On the road it is comforting to see them as beacons, assurances of home, and it is true that if your car broke down not many along here would turn you away. And yet you know that if these kitchens and living rooms could be hoisted onto stages in theatres, the lives revealed would not seem so fortunate, so safe from the night. You want to believe that your own life would not look so bad up there, but you know that your solitude would then be no protection. The audience would have to be patient, but the revelations would come.

A hundred kilometres and you pull in under a revolving blue neon sign that says,

BOBS' SERVICE
GAS & COF EE BAR
OPEN PEN OP

The place could be a two-suite motel. It stands across a bare-earth parking lot with so many and such regular depressions that under the neon it looks like a blue mattress. You pull up to the pumps and turn off the engine. Orange plastic curtains hang in the window of the coffee shop. You can see arborite tables, serviette dispensers, dark-red plastic ketchup containers. No sign of life. You want to drive on, but you could run out of gas. You blow the horn. Eventually, in your side mirror, you see an attendant wearing a dirty white waiter's jacket. In the centre of his forehead is a mole half the size of a dime. On his way to your window he lightly flicks a dish towel at the side of your car. You roll down the window and tell him to fill it up with regular and check the oil. When he sees your face he does a double take, places both hands on your door, and leans on it with locked elbows. He is pale and badly shaven. His nose is unusually high and small. There is a certain unfocussed quality about his expression that gives him a look of congenital retardation. His hair is spiky. He is about thirty years old.

"Hi Cort," he says. "When'd you get out?"

"Pardon?"

"Where'd you get the car?"

"It's my car. You don't know me."

This he takes as a great joke. "Ha!" he shouts and slaps your door with the dish towel.

Again you tell him to fill it up with regular and check the oil.

Poker-faced now, with deliberate gestures, he spreads the dish towel on the hood of your car and goes through his pockets for a small, flat container and a larger cylindrical one, both of which he places on the dish towel, lowering his face to within a few inches of the hood. With his left hand he opens the smaller container while sucking his right forefinger. He places a contact lens on his tongue and moves it around his mouth for a few seconds before spitting it onto the tip of his right forefinger, holding his right eye open with the middle fingers of both hands. As he does this he grimaces with concentration, and you notice that his teeth are bad. He hesitates. He returns to your window grasping the contact lens between his thumb and forefinger.

173

"How come, Cort, every time I try to put in my contacts a wind comes up?"

As he says this you feel a light breeze against your face. "I'm not Cort," you say. "Could you just give me some gas."

Carefully he returns the lens to its case, gathers up both containers in the dish towel, and says, "Sure. Lemme unlock the pump."

He disappears inside. After a full minute by your watch you start the engine.

"Hey, Cort! I thought you wanted a gas-up!"

He is at your door wearing mirrored sunglasses. You turn off the engine and roll down the window.

"See better now?" you ask.

"Oh sure. Premium, eh?"

"Regular, and check the oil."

While he is doing the windshield you ask who Cort is.

He leans over close to the glass and says, "Cort is *you*!" Then he laughs.

After he has slammed the hood he comes to your window and looks at the credit card you are holding out to him. "Hey Cort," he says. "You know the boss don't take plastic money." His manner is a shy blend of embarrassment and reproach.

You give him two twenties.

As he hands you your change, he says, "No honey along eh, Cort?"

"Afraid not."

"Nice night, though."

"Yes it is." You start the engine.

"No bugs."

"Not yet." You shift into gear.

He leans closer to the window, confidential. "I'm surprised at you taking regular, Cort."

"Thanks," you say, letting out the clutch.

"*When'd you get it cut?*" he suddenly shouts, gripping then letting go of the doorhandle, and as you pull away he calls, "*Hey, nice haircut, Cort!*" and stands watching until you are back on the highway.

You had intended to wash and have a coffee and something to eat in there, but you did not want to listen to more of that. You wonder who Cort is and how little you would need to look like him to confuse somebody that stupid. In the rearview the blue sign shifts sideways and disappears. The only visible light now is your high beams. The road is deserted. You are hungry and tired.

As you start up a long grade you see what looks like a white sign on the shoulder, and then you realize it is a hitchhiker. The best reasons are the ones for not picking up hitchhikers, and you almost never do, but then you almost always feel guilty. This time you decide that you will stop if it is a woman. A honey who will change your life. Who will let you take her to the city and overestimate her distinguishing details.

But it is not a honey. It is a man in baggy trousers and a loose white collarless top like a nightshirt. His hair is cropped and fair. Even at a distance he looks familiar. You strain to see his face ... In fact, he looks like a bleached-out version of—

Was that *Cort*?

Was he staring as hard at you as—?

Or was that the look of any hitchhiker stranded past dark in the middle of nowhere? He must have been freezing in those clothes. How could you not stop?

You *have* to stop—

But inertia is sweet, and it grows sweeter by the second.

Too late now. Best to just keep moving.

What were you thinking of? He looked like a mental patient.

You drive down into farmland. When you enter a brightly lit strip of service stations, fast food outlets, and boarded-up

175

blueberry stalls, you pull into a 24-hour coffee and doughnut place. As you walk past the cash register on your way to the washroom you are half aware that someone down the counter with a cup of coffee at his mouth has turned to watch. You keep going. The washroom is the kind where they pile extra deodorant pucks in the urinals instead of cleaning them. But there is hot water and a mirror, so after you wash you examine the face in it.

Who is this? You make a grin. A mirror has got to be the worst way in the world to find out.

At the counter you order a coffee and a grilled danish. The waitress—she should have been your hitchhiker—does not, however, know what a grilled danish is. When you explain, she replies that she is not allowed to use the grill. You ask her why there is a grill and why it is hot, and she shrugs. She is not defensive. At first her eyes say, *Please, I just work here*, and then they light up, and she tells you there's a microwave. You do not like microwaves. You have a chocolate doughnut, a dish of ice cream, and a coffee. You remember that the person who watched you come in will have been listening to all this. When you glance along the counter at him he is watching the girl. He does not look like you. In a booth behind you two men in their fifties wearing Cat caps are talking about a car accident.

"Junk," the one who was there is saying. "They were putting them in bags."

Outside as you are unlocking your car you realize that someone is watching you across the roof. When you look up, he glances away, over at the highway, where a truck is pulling out, and says, "Going to the city?"

The profile is yours. It is what you see in the triple mirror in a men's shop. And now he is fully twisted around to watch the truck, and you are looking at the back of your own head, like the Magritte. It is something from a dream.

"Sorry, I don't take hitchhikers," you say quickly.

"Is my thumb out?" He has swung back around and is looking at his thumb. What you see is not what you saw just now in the mirror but a bad likeness, the muscles all wrong. "I am not hitching, I am praying for a ride." He has placed his hands together and set them on the roof of your car. "Can't you see I am also freezing to death?" He shifts from foot to foot and shivers. "*Please!*"

Why do they pick on you?

And then you think, It's only life. Better than old tapes and country radio. Your city break can start here.

To smooth the shift from no to yes, you ask if he is hungry.

"No," he says and glowers.

"Let me buy you a hamburger and Coke or something, and then we can leave."

He turns on his heel and goes inside.

When you stand next to him in front of the doughnut display he is exactly your height, and you are surprised that no one looks twice. They must think you are brothers. There are of course no hamburgers, only doughnuts. "I'll take a cinnamon," he tells the waitress, "a chocolate, two cherry fills, and a cream. And a large Coke, please. And, uh"—she hesitates, waiting—"my favourite night-time snack: *a roll in bed with a little honey*!" He winks and does a dance. The waitress smiles. Now people are looking twice.

And now you do not want them to think you are brothers. His features seem a lot softer than your own, certainly paler.

The waitress rustles the bag of doughnuts. "That's four-fifty." As you pay, the hitchhiker takes the bag and the Coke and steps outside. When you reach your car he is standing on the passenger side eating a doughnut and stamping his feet.

"Are you Cort?" you ask across the car roof, feeling foolish.

He rolls his eyes. "Court? What Court? Supreme? Ten-

177

nis? Small Claims? Motor? Hey, *you* must be Motor! Would you just let me into the car please, Motor? I am freezing!"

You get in and unlock his door. He climbs in quickly and clicks into his seatbelt. "What kind of a name is Court?" he asks.

"Forget it."

You should not have picked him up. As you pull onto the highway, he goes through an obsessive, elaborate ritual of settling in: tapping his plastic shoes on the mat, tugging his pants at the knees, double-checking his seatbelt, shifting his hips, clearing his throat, repeatedly jerking his head to the right. And then he is staring at you. "Let's get one thing straight right away, Motor. You and me are two completely different propositions. There is no need to pretend that we have a single thing in common, and I do not plan to be your cheap entertainment for the next two hours. You'll have to get your spontaneous combustion elsewheres. I have better things to do with my awjays."

He grins and takes a big bite of doughnut. "If you want sounds, turn on the radio." He pronounces it to rhyme with *Daddy-o.*

"OK with me," you say.

He looks at you. "It's not as if we're long lost brothers who have a lot to talk about. I bet you don't even have one."

"That's right. Do you?"

"No, no. I'm just like you." He laughs softly and takes a long drink of Coke.

You laugh too. You must be relieved.

He is looking at you again. And though you know it's the worst possible thing you could do, you say, "So you think we look a little alike?"

At first the question seems to stun him. Suddenly he twists the rearview mirror to study his face, then leans across and studies yours. "You and me? Are you serious?"

You readjust the mirror, so he slouches to see into the one on the passenger side.

"I don't think I look like you at all," he says. "Do you really think that?"

You don't answer.

"Hey! Earth to Motor! Come in Motor!"

"Do you want to get out of the car?"

"What's your first name?"

You tell him your first name.

"Huh," he says. "Second?"

You tell him.

He shakes his head. Looks hard out his window. He says something.

"Same name?" you say.

He nods.

"Listen," you say. "Suddenly I don't feel like going through this. Maybe you should get out of the car."

"Here—?"

"Next stop."

He is quiet for a long time. When you smell something, you look over and he is huddled against the door. "Where are you taking us?" he asks in a small voice. He has shit his pants.

"Oh Jesus." You reach into the back seat for a newspaper, swerve into the other lane. "Here"—but he thinks you are going to hit him with it; his forearms slide up over his face, his fists ball at the top of his head, and he cowers deeper into the corner—"put this under you. Lift your ass." He has begun to shake. "Look, I'm not going to hurt you. Give me your Coke, you'll spill it." You set the Coke on the dash.

His eyes are not focussed. "You can't," he whispers.

"Can't what." His trembling is getting worse. He's going to get shit all over the seat. "Listen. In the trunk there's a pair of old pants—"

You are coming up fast on some kind of backhoe. It is

179

signalling right, swinging wide for the turn. You pull out to pass.

"Listen," you say. "Would you really rather get out right here?"

His answer is too soft to make out. You lean over to hear what it was. Now he says something like a sigh that you can't hear at all.

"Pardon? You're *who*? Oh yeah?" You glance at your watch. "Terrific. Just great. I'm honoured. Look, if you could help me get this newspaper under—"

Without braking, that backhoe is turning *left*, not swinging wide at all. You lean on the horn, accelerating. You move to the shoulder, but the shoulder is sand and deep gravel. It slows you. The backhoe keeps coming, following through on a quick, tight turn. You see its headlights sweep a scatter of white rectangles on your left like blank playing cards stuck in the earth at angles. You would choose the ditch but you are too close to the banking of the lane and the black zero mouth of a culvert.

And now you have all the time in the world. Adrenaline is coursing through your body like fresh water. You see that the backhoe is a John Deere and that it is entering a cemetery. The playing cards are gravestones luminous in its headlights. Some are eclipsed by blue spruce. There is a wire fence with new, upright posts. An owl is perched on one of the gravestones; its eyes are yellow light. It blinks once, so leisurely, and you understand that this slow blaze is the intelligence of owls. You see that the cemetery gate stands open, that the cemetery is just a fenced-off acre some farmer must plough around. A place for dead people, or what is left of them. You see plastic flowers, wreaths.

In wonder you look to the driver of that two-ton wall of steel that your car is about to explode into, and you see that it is an old woman with thick grey hair twisted and knotted

down the back of her jacket. Across the shoulder against a
reflecting silver ground is the name *Eileen*. She is wearing
black trousers and muddy red rubber boots. Her face was
once handsome but now it is toothless and collapsed, and she
has swung in her seat to curse you, in an effortless stream.
You wonder if this could be your honey, grown old and
eloquent, like a character in a play. Your hitchhiker is right
there, at your ear, and you think the voice must be his, in the
full fluency of his terror.

WHEN SHE WAS GONE

The nurse in charge of Snider's wing is not the one you spoke to on the phone last night. She knows him though, everybody knows him. He's in the common room, sitting at an arborite table talking to a boy six or seven. According to his file, Snider has just turned seventy-four, but he looks more like sixty. His white hair is cropped, and he wears glasses now, to correct that squint. He is cleanshaven and pinker, fuller in the face.

"Oh look," the nurse whispers. "He's with the Gein boy. They're great pals," and in her nurse's singsong she calls, "Mr. Snider! You got a visitor!"

Snider takes one sharp look at you and says, "Eddie, go find your mama."

"Hello, Gordon," you say, and as you pull up a chair you remember the moment from twenty-five years ago, Snider across the table, the weight of the handcuffs in your palm.

* * *

It would not be true to say I am not bothered by the things that were done. I have thought about them a good deal, not worried so much as tried to understand. I would say that blowing through the world is a wind of destruction. People huddle and say, You can know this, you can't know that. Others see the thing for what it is: a simple matter of salvage.

* * *

A mile south of the Third Line, where the dump road cut off through diseased maples to loop at the edge of a trench bottomed with garbage under raw plywood signs in black aerosol that said *Dump Hear*, *Brush Only*, and *Mettal and HouseHold*, Cheryl Deinert swung the pickup into a lane that wound another mile through rock and low bush. If she kept going, the lane would cross a hydro cut line where defoliants had turned green balsams to burnt sienna, but she said,

"We'll leave the truck before the cut and circle the dump on foot. The Snider place is half a mile past it down the Third."

There was no reply. This had been discussed. Like guerrillas they had studied a map.

"Hey," said Vicky Armitage from under the dash. "Can I come out yet?"

"Come out, come out," Cheryl said.

When they were planning this, Vicky had argued it would be crazy to walk a mile through this bush carrying two-and-a-half gallon tanks, but really they had no choice. Too much dump traffic past the Snider place.

The trek turned out to be only tiring. It was too late in the year for bugs, the ground was rock, and once they were past the ravens, the stink, and the invisible bears of the dump, they cut back close to the concession road and so did not, as Vicky had predicted they would, miss their target and wander off into seven thousand acres of crown bush.

It was Lynn who first glimpsed the tin roof through a screen of spruce. From there they could see the weedless, perfect circle of a pond so blue it should have had snow-white geese swimming in it; a cedar-railed compound containing a somehow orderly arrangement of damaged car and truck bodies; segregated engine parts; neat stacks of tires; rows of doors, bumpers, fenders; behind the house a freshly-painted outhouse; and the house itself: two storeys of faded Insulbrick with narrow windows.

Attached to the back of the house was a new addition, painted red.

"Neat as a pin," Vicky said.

"No flies on Gordon Snider." Cheryl indicated the outhouse. "Funny no plumbing."

"Maybe he didn't shit much."

"Grass needs cutting," Lynn noticed. "Where's the animals?"

"Impounded. He won't be coming back."

"You hope."

They stared at the silent property.

"Hey," Vicky said. "Maybe this is going too far."

Immediately Cheryl pushed a set of keys into Vicky's hand. "Vick. Don't worry. Go back to the truck. You already did more than enough. See you in one hour at the most. You too, Lynn."

"Which window," Lynn said.

Cheryl turned back to the house. "The one on the left—"

"I'll pass it in to you," Lynn said.

Vicky returned the keys. "I'm the one gets lost at the A & P, remember?"

"You wouldn't find that truck any better with me along," Lynn said kindly.

Taking care to keep the house between themselves and the road, they carried the tanks to the back window. Tied to the knob of the addition door was a red police tag that said, "Break Enter & Theft of a dwelling could result in life imprisonment."

"Christ. That's worse than Snider got."

"Know what?" Cheryl said. "This addition's got no windows."

"What if there's an alarm?" Vicky asked.

"Why should there be an alarm?" Cheryl unfolded a Swiss army knife and slit the window screen. She pounded one side of the frame with a rock until the thing splintered and fell in. Lynn and Vicky made a stirrup by locking fingers, and Cheryl climbed inside.

"More guts than I'll ever have," Vicky said. She was showing Lynn her hands, which were shaking.

Cheryl stuck her head out the window. Briefly she examined a bit of sun-stained curtain before she looked at them again. "Won't be long," she said and was gone.

* * *

She was a good woman, one of the best. She was good in every way. A little stern maybe. I hated the way she suffered at the end there. The strokes and that. A man could turn away from God. Still, He knows best. Sometimes in certain sleep zones I would hear her voice. Once I had a dream about a forest that had the tops of all the trees sheared and vultures watching down from the branches that were left. It was hard to live in that house. I had plenty of spells of the blues.

* * *

Cheryl stepped aside from the window to let more light in and wait for her eyes to adjust to the darkness. Through the wall to the left she could hear rats scrabbling. It was a narrow parlour she was in, as deep as the house and as still and abandoned as the yard outside. The air seemed fifty years old. Faded wallpaper, linoleum, hooked rugs. A stuffed chair and a sofa, soft with dust. In flight along the right-hand wall were five silver geese, jig-sawed from plywood. Otherwise the walls held faded prints in pasteboard frames: *Northern Lake Sunset*, *Storm at Sea*, *Parliament Buildings Ottawa*. Cheryl tried a lamp and a wall switch: nothing. She crossed to the one door, took a breath, and opened it—on a wall of plywood. Police, she thought at first, but the plywood was not new and dust lay in the corners of the space between it and the door. Must have been up before the police came through; they had put it back.

She returned to the window to tell Lynn and Vicky what

185

to expect, went back and kicked at the plywood with the heel of her boot. Nailed tight. She hit it with her shoulder, and again, harder. The nails shrieked free, and the panel fell against the opposite wall of a narrow hallway. To the right was the front door, to the left the second floor stairs. They too had been sealed, once. This time the police had pried off the plywood sheet and left it leaning against the wall. The floor had been carefully swept.

Cheryl climbed the stairs. Along the front of the house was a bedroom—his mother's. The bible by the bed, the hairbrush on the dresser, were half buried in dust. Except for the police again—scuffs in the dust, a drawer standing open—this room, like the living room, must not have been touched since the woman's death. Same with the bathroom. So he did have plumbing, had boarded it off too. The third and last upstairs room was abandoned, with hangers and dustballs scattered across the floor and a door standing open on an empty closet.

Downstairs, on the other side of the front hallway from the long parlour, was a cramped room containing a La-Z-Boy, a bed, a bureau, a wardrobe. The bureau was empty. In the wardrobe were wire hangers, on the walls pictures of movie stars, publicity stills, the kind that come in Woolworth frames: Ginger Rogers, Mitzi Gaynor, Judy Garland. In this room the floor was patterned with dust in a way that said things had been moved out. A lot of things. Police again.

The kitchen was a darkness into which light came only from a small window over the sink; a bigger window had been closed off by the new addition. The kitchen was where the rats had been busy: cupboard and pantry contents strewn across the floor.

The back door opened into the deeper darkness of the addition. Cheryl felt her way to the door next to where Lynn and Vicky waited, called to them, and unlocked it.

"Don't scare us like that," Vicky said as they crowded in with the light.

When Cheryl turned she saw a room painted red, a Milky Way of gold foil stars across the ceiling. She saw an iron clothesrack without hangers, a full-length mirror unsilvered along the edges, a wood cookstove, dark stains on the floor.

"Hey, come on guys," she said. "Let's just do it," and moved to push Lynn and Vicky back outside.

But Vicky had crouched to raise a floorboard.

"What's this?" she said, reaching to lift something into the light. It flew from her fingers, and she was screaming.

"Right," Cheryl said, shoving her. "Everybody out. Just get me the gasoline."

* * *

Once I did consider getting married. But I couldn't think how to start things rolling. We skated on the river in those days. "Hey, let's go skate, Mary" (or Beth, or whatever) stayed stuck on my tongue all one winter there. I never ice-skated in my life. Still haven't. One time my mother said to me, "If a woman is good enough for intercourse, she is good enough for marriage." That's pretty true I guess. Doris Cooney? She was nice all right, even if she did have that tongue. Some people used to take her for the resemblance of my mother. Her height and everything was different, though maybe she had resemblance in the cheekbones. But my mother sure never talked like that one.

* * *

On a cool April night, seventeen months before the Snider house burned, a Ford pickup splashed across a bare-earth parking lot to nose against a low windowless building along-side a Dodge sedan with its headlights burning amber. In neon lasso by the door of the building was the name *Coun-*

tryman Restaurant and Lounge. The sky was black with moving cloud, but the night below was as dank and still as a basement. Everywhere except near the highway, where the diesel vapours drifted and eddied, and by the ventilation fan at the back of the building where two ten-year-old girls had dropped their bicycles and pressed their mouths against the mesh to get drunk on the fumes, the air had the perfume on it of wet balsam.

Inside the lounge an obese man named Orest Thoms presided over the one occupied table. He sat tipped complacently toward a smaller, crewcut version of himself. This was his nephew Sy. Sy was hunched on the edge of his chair with his hands on his knees and with his elbows pivoted forward in a way suggesting that at any moment he would jump up and rush out. The third man, Albert Fennick, was gaunt and hollow-eyed. At those junctures Albert might feel himself called upon to speak or laugh he would cough instead down into his windbreaker.

The door opened, and the owner of the Ford pickup entered. Gordon Snider was a fox-faced man with a cast to his right eye that gave him an appearance of oblique private scrutiny. He was wearing a John Deere cap, a yellow plaid shirt buttoned to the neck, high-cut olive-green workpants, and running shoes. He nodded to the waitress who stood by the cash.

"Hey Snider," Thoms called. "Are you going to be sociable and hear some intelligent comment on what's been going on around here lately or sit by yourself and learn nothing?"

"The only thing I'll learn from you, Thoms," said Gordon Snider as he walked past Thoms' table, "is how to be a fool." Thoms made I-told-you-so eyes for the others. "Just being friendly, Gordon."

Snider did not reply. He sat down at a table by himself, his back to the others. When the waitress came over he said,

"Little bit on the damp side."

"Almost prefer more snow than this piss," she replied.

"I'll have the hot turkey on white, mashed potatoes with a large Coke. No ice in the Coke."

* * *

There is a common streak to most women that my mother did not approve. I do not mind it so much myself, except that I wonder if their own thinking is there, or are they just trying to be like the rest. My standards got set too high maybe. It was a curse and an honour to know her. My mother was so intelligent you could never exactly tell what she meant. I know I got my brains from always trying to figure that one out.

* * *

The same morning a check-out girl found Snider's friend Little Jimmy stuffed in the shopping cart in the A & P lot, Doris Cooney went missing without a trace except some blood on the floors and walls. That night the Chief still wasn't back from holiday, so you drove out to Snider's place on your own. It was one of those black Spring nights. He wasn't there and you didn't go in, but coming back into town you spotted his pickup outside the Countryman.

Snider's neighbour he had the feud going with, Orest Thoms, was there with his nephew Sy and Sick Albert Fennick. Snider's latest grievance against Thoms was that Thoms was paying somebody that Snider also had a grievance against to take his hay off. Snider was sitting with his back to Orest's table as if Orest did not exist, arranging golf tees in one of those little wooden triangles while he ate.

You sat down across from Snider and said, "Gordon, I have to take a drive over to your place."

"Have to, eh McIntyre? Then I guess you better go ahead. But you won't find what you're looking for."

189

"I'd like you to come with me."

"You can see I'm eating. You go along. I'll wait right here."

"Give me your keys. Truck keys too."

He placed them on the table, watching you.

"You're just a dumb lunk, McIntyre," he said as you stood up. "You don't know what you're in for."

"Don't threaten me, Snider."

It wasn't a threat.

* * *

I always was one to know. Now you see it now you don't. If a person can't understand how a thing works how can he know what it is? Life isn't pictures on a wall however it might seem sometimes. A person has to walk in and wade around. Get their hands dirty if that is what it takes. Otherwise they might as well be asleep like everybody else. One day some people look around, say Pinch Me, and want to know.

* * *

When you got back to the lounge you were still shaking. In the parking lot you threw up again, to the amazement of a couple of girls standing with their bicycles.

Snider was inside, as promised, drinking coffee, playing the golf tee game. Orest, Sy, and Sick Albert were also still there, waiting to see what was going on.

You sat down across from Snider, as before.

He watched you, amused by your condition.

"Put your hands on the table," you said.

He placed both fists flat on the table, wrists together. Small hands. He smiled. "Pretty bad, was it?"

You could hardly get the handcuffs on him for shaking. The others were watching closely.

Suddenly Snider shouted, "*Thoms!*"

You jumped, everybody jumped.

"You talking to me, Gordon?" Orest said.

"You didn't leave your lights on, did you, Thoms?"

"Shut up, Snider!" you said.

"Don't think so, Gordon," Thoms said. "Did I?"

"Maybe you did."

"If so, thanks a lot for telling me right away."

Thoms was feeling for his keys.

"Let's go," you said.

"Maybe you should turn them off," Snider told Thoms as he stood up. "If you can find your keys, that is."

"Awful thoughtful of you, Gordon—" Thoms stopped patting his pockets. "Hey Gordon. What's those pretty bracelets Doug's put on you there?"

"Maybe you locked them inside the car."

Thoms was back checking his jacket pockets while watching the handcuffs as you walked Snider towards the door. You were almost abreast of Thoms when Snider's fists flicked up and something slapped hard into Thoms' chest and dropped to the floor. A set of car keys.

When Orest stooped for them, Snider made a kick at his face. You grabbed a handful of shirt and carried him straight out to the cruiser and threw him into the back. He was light as a cat.

Outside, on the edge of the parking lot, when they saw who it was, the two young girls laid down their bikes and stood with their arms around each other's necks. In the rearview Gordon Snider twisted in his seat to give those girls a fierce, happy smile. It was still fading when he turned back around, the radiance of his pleasure.

* * *

As I told them over and over, my girls all come from elsewheres. The Cooney woman was pure accident, a stroke of bad fortune. Something ordained to happen. The time comes it comes. There was no intention. It puzzles me. Even now it seems like a dream, impossible. No, anybody did it, that was somebody else. I definitely didn't that I know of. Drifters would be my guess.

* * *

The night before Doug McIntyre arrested Gordon Snider, Gordon and his friend Little Jimmy were out in Snider's Ford pickup driving west out of town. This was the first time since October Snider had fetched Jimmy from Mrs. Afelski's and taken him home for a meal. But tonight Jimmy had not been himself. Instead of eating his stew he laid his arms on the table and rested his head now on one elbow and now on the other, sighing and yawning. When Snider, who as usual had promised Mrs. Afelski to have Jimmy back by eleven and was conscious of the work that lay before them, asked what the matter was, Jimmy would only say that he was not hungry. In three years Jimmy had never not been hungry for one of Gordon Snider's meals. Finished his own, chewing gum, Snider sat tipped back in his chair watching Jimmy poke at his food.

Later, out in the truck, Jimmy whispered, "'S too cold, Gordon."

"No bugs yet," Snider replied. "Ground's fresh-broke as well."

On arrival Jimmy refused to get out of the truck. Snider had to haul him out and press his fingers around the shovel.

"They get whole carloads of snivellers in here, Jimmy," he told him. "Make a difference."

At the site Jimmy stood and gazed at the gravestone. "What's her name?" he asked finally, wiping his eyes.

"Fobbs."

There was a pause.

"*Mary-Ellen!*" Jimmy cried, in a kind of anguish. "Mary-Ellen *Fobbs*! She worked at the Roxy!"

192

"That was another one. This one here was a whore out at the Fifth Wheel. Cancer victim."

Jimmy kept shaking his head.

"Jimmy, do you realize how many she-Fobbses they have in this township?"

"Gordon, it's *her*!"

Snider repositioned his cap on his head. "Jimmy, am I your best friend or what?"

Jimmy was sobbing. "You can't if you're not Jesus Christ Our Lord and Saviour in Heaven!"

"Can't what?"

Jimmy did not reply.

Snider put an arm around his shoulder. He whispered in his ear. "You been talking to that new minister, Jimmy?" The shovel fell from Jimmy's hand.

"*Pick it up.*"

"Don't have to, Gordon. You're my best friend on the face of the earth, but Jesus is my Lord and Saviour in Heaven!"

Jimmy turned and started back to the truck.

Snider used the shovel he held in his own hands to hit Jimmy across the back of the head. He knelt at Jimmy's ear.

"And here I bought you new runners."

Jimmy moaned.

Snider dragged Jimmy to the truck and propped him in the passenger's seat. The shovels he had to go back for.

* * *

The thing about salvage its time is after. Real life happens right now or it doesn't happen. In real life there is a person behind those eyes a man had better face with all the brains he's got because if he fails to, you better be careful. Hurricanes and ruby shoes is one thing. Taking them live is another.

* * *

Little Jimmy stirred when Snider pulled up in front of Cooney's General Store.

"Wha—?" Jimmy said as Snider got his rifle from the rack behind the seat.

"Almost there. Wait in the truck."

Doris Cooney came through a curtained doorway behind a long counter that ran the length of her store. She was a tall woman with painful hips that caused her to walk with a rolling, nautical motion. When she saw Snider she stopped to consider him the way she might have considered a drunk.

Snider nodded affably and wandered down a far aisle studying buns and sugar loaves. When he reached the end he looked up and saw her watching him in a convex mirror. He must have known that she could see the rifle, which he held in close to the right side of his body, because he came around the display rack with the barrel in his fist and leaned the weapon against the counter in front of her saying,

"Don't need this to shop, I guess."

"Early for bear," Mrs. Cooney said.

"Is that right."

Mrs. Cooney did not reply.

"Little bit on the cool side though," Snider said.

"What are you doing in here?"

"Any bandages?"

Snider touched his palms lightly against the edge of the counter.

Mrs. Cooney shook her head.

"Bandaids?"

"No."

Snider ran his fingers along the edge of the cash register, admiring the old machine.

"Sure like to get my hands on one of these beauties some day. How's about eye-oh-dine?"

"Go to the drugstore."

"Peroxide?"

"You got exactly ten minutes."

"For what."

Snider's eyes indicated the cash register.

"How does this work. Pretty complicated, I guess."

"Drugstore closes in ten minutes, as you well know."

Snider nodded. His eyes went to the curtains she had come through.

"The thing is, Doris, this is a first aid emergency—"

"Why?" Mrs. Cooney was interested. "What's happened?"

"My pet bear just got hit by a lad with a shovel."

"Bear?"

"Kind of shaggy? Walks on all fours?"

Mrs. Cooney's eyes were grey and cold.

Snider had been scratching at the back of his head, pushing his cap forward until the peak was all the way over his eyes. Now he pushed it high on his head and said, "Come on, Doris. Let's have a look."

"I don't keep bandages."

"You should."

Snider gripped the edge of the counter tightly, let go.

"You know," he said and grew thoughtful. "I go into a store and a woman comes out from someplace—I don't know what it is—I just have to find out how she's got it all arranged back in there. Little Barry the Bear can bleed to death all over my truck for what you or me care, Doris. I just want to crawl into your medicine chest and take a poke around."

"Get out of my store."

Snider seemed to consider this. Then he said, "I am driving along with Barry. He's my bear. Blood everywhere. Damn kids and their shovels. We see this here big brick house. Store. Whatever it is. I see it. Too much of the plasma ratazzma in

195

Barry's eyes to see a damn thing. And this house here has this store sort of on the front but also sort of on the inside. And out of deeper inside this store comes a woman. Name? Doris Cooney. I know that, I knew it all my life, but who exactly is Doris Cooney?"

"Stop this right now. If your—"

"*Mother*, Doris? Are you going to start to talk about my mother? Go ahead. She talked enough about you. In fact she told me just about everything, and it was a very complicated story, Doris, you've had such a complicated life, but she never told me the answer to one question:"—here Snider reached out as if to finger the material of Mrs. Cooney's sleeve—"What exactly is it like inside this here sensible old nylon dress?"

"Get your hands off me!"

Snider nodded sleepily.

"How does it go together, all this here skin and bone."

He reached to touch her flesh, but Mrs. Cooney was out of range, backed to the wall.

Snider picked up the rifle by holding the tip of the barrel between the thumb and forefinger of his left hand. He continued to talk.

"What's it like. That's what I want to know."

Snider held the rifle high. He let it drop and caught it in his right hand.

At the trial Snider insisted he was only fooling, it was an accident. Whatever it was, Snider, "in a kind of a dream," was immediately over the counter to drag the body outside and roll it into the box of the pickup. Next he was back for the cash register, which he emptied before he carried it too out to the truck.

As Snider knelt on the seat of the cab to fasten the rifle in its rack, he said, "Now Jimmy, see what you got me up to with your Jesus Lord and Saviour in Heaven?"

But Jimmy, who had a cracked skull and a brain slowly filling up with blood, was slumped against the dash and did not hear.

* * *

Everybody has a place for salvage, whatever they might say or act like, and they watch over this place from day to day, protect it at any cost maybe. Different salvage might come and go, but it's always the same. A picture in a book or a magazine, a memory with a shine on it, or an actual souvenir of a person, it's a changing dream, that's all. Everywhere you look these days salvage is on display. It's like hair in a locket. Everybody knows this, everybody does it.

* * *

Jimmy's reluctance to help Gordon Snider had its origin the previous time he had been invited to dinner, four months earlier. On that evening a massive surprise snowstorm not only prevented them from going out but prevented Snider from delivering Jimmy back to Mrs. Afelski's that same night. And so after Snider had given Jimmy his meal and beaten him at checkers, he put him to bed, in a fold-up cot in Snider's own room. When Jimmy complained that he could not sleep without a light, Snider assured him there would be plenty from the snow. But there was no light from the snow, so Jimmy tiptoed to the door and opened it, to see Snider clearing the table from dinner and filling the sink to do the dishes. Jimmy left the door ajar for the light from the kitchen and fell asleep. Sometime later he woke up in darkness afraid. For a long while he listened but heard nothing. He crept to Snider's bed; it was still made. The door to the kitchen had been closed. Cautiously he opened it. The kitchen was dark, but light came from around the edges of the door to the new addition, where Jimmy had never been allowed. He crept across the kitchen to the addition door and looked in.

What Jimmy saw was Gordon Snider sitting naked in a chair, his back turned, leaning over to wrap his legs. As Jimmy watched, Snider went on to wrap his arms. The material was tawny and soft like oiled leather; he was using his teeth to fasten it with string. On the table beside Snider more of the tan stuff was laid out, in the shape of a girdle. When Snider stood to reach for something, half-turning, Jimmy ducked out of sight and hurried back to his cot, where he lay thinking about what he had just seen: Gordon Snider's eyes outlined in black, his lips in red.

After a while Jimmy was no longer so sure that he had not been dreaming when he saw Gordon Snider looking so much like the devil. Again he listened for the sound of Snider's breathing and heard nothing. Again he crept out of the room and across the kitchen to the addition. This time what he saw was a creature in a black dress and bare feet, with bracelets that jangled. It had smooth tan skin and it prowled stiffly, like an animal awkward in a cage, tossing its shining hair. Sometimes it stopped to peer around into a long mirror at the hem of the dress, and the dress swirled and lifted as it turned.

Back in his bed Jimmy did not know what he had seen, but he knew something that it didn't know: It was not a woman. And when he knew that he understood. Gordon Snider was not Jesus. If Jesus had brought it back it would know what it was.

* * *

Sometimes a person might even think this whole world's a house of cards of pure salvage. And then there's TV and that's all it is, from start to finish. And everybody knows and nobody talks about it. As if the truth will bring too much down. It's like somebody speaks out about life and people say, What's your beef? As if this was treason. Get on side, mister. Think the good things. But what if some people's salvage has more of the stink of truth to it? What if some people's has been required from Day One to do more duty? What if some people are not satisfied with the usual apportion of knowledge?

* * *

The front door wasn't locked. You switched on the light, a forty-watt bulb on a wire. The front hall was filled with junk, in boxes and barrels. There were piles of clothes, papers, magazines, books. You could hardly squeeze in. You stumbled through the junk towards a door off the hall to the right. The one across from it had a sheet of greasy plywood nailed over it. What the hell? And so did the door straight ahead, probably to upstairs. The open door on the right led into Snider's own room, maybe eight by ten. There wasn't much light. Your eyes took some time to adjust. Aside from a foot-wide passageway from the bed to the kitchen, it was the same in there. Papers, books, rags, boxes. Junk to the ceiling, almost. A lot of it was old clothes. There was a stack of worn-out overalls four feet high. On the floor by the side of the bed was a pound coffee can filled to the brim with wads of gum. It was like the lair of an animal. A funny smell.

As soon as you saw the first one you saw them everywhere: bones, big raw bones with strips of withered fat and muscle still attached. There was a chair in the corner, made out of bones.

You made your way to the kitchen. It was the same in there. Something—probably seeing such a thing amongst all that junk—made you open a hatbox. Inside was a woman's head. After that it was all women. There was a bag made out of a pair of nylon underpants with half a dozen vulvas in it, one of them painted gold, a red ribbon tied to it, two turning green. Another head in a burlap sack in a cupboard. An apron with nipples stitched in a zero. On the wall, masks made from women's skinned faces, stretched on big crochet hoops. A

199

heart in a saucepan on the stove. An ear ashtray, a cigarette stubbed in it.

In the back room you found the remains of Doris Cooney. He'd slipped a four-inch diameter wooden rod through the tendons at the back of her ankles and hung her upside down, headless, slit open, dressed out like a deer. The head you found in a bag under a mattress. You knew where to look because the back room was unheated, the mattress was steaming. There was an iron clothesrack. On the hangers, slips and dresses and the skins of women's torsos, tanned and oiled, slit down the front, with holes where the arms used to be. String for lacing up.

* * *

All in all I'm happy enough how things turned out. This place suits me fine. An institution's just a bunch of people doing their job along with the grain and against the odds. Some of these nurses just do what they're told, but some of them are pretty complicated. It's a full-time occupation to understand what is going on inside their heads, and the turnover's good. You get one figured, soon enough there's a new one to start on. It's a good life.

* * *

One day you call over to the hospital, and the nurse says, "Gordon Snider? He's right here."

As if he's been waiting by the phone for twenty-five years. "Would you like to speak to him?"

"No, no. I'll just show up. What's your visiting hours?"

So you show up and you talk to Snider and after that you go and see the head of the place, a guy with the most creased face you ever saw, sloppy grey hair, skin that clay pallor of two packs a day. As he's ushering you out of his office he takes you aside.

"What I'm saying, Mr. McIntyre, it's not that there aren't reasons for the way he turned out, a logic, his mother, and so forth. I'm not denying it's an interesting case. But I'd want to question very closely indeed anybody who'd try to generalize from it. This is a very disturbed individual, and that's the bottom line. We've got plenty of his type in here, I'm unhappy to say, of both sexes. You understand what I'm getting at? You take my advice, you'll go home and put this whole thing out of your mind."

"I thought I did. It came back."

"People retire, and the past will do that. Especially after an active life like your own. The point is, a man like Snider, you'd be better off rummaging through garbage cans, you know what I'm saying?"

He starts you walking again.

"You play golf, Mr. McIntyre?"

"Not really. I never had the time."

"You have to make time. I play every day I can."

He stops again, and this time there's a hand on your shoulder.

"It's a fine game, McIntyre, a man's game. Precision. Patience. I recommend it."

You're standing at the front doors, and he's sighting through the glass down the softest, greenest, most dew-shining fairway there ever was on this earth. It's the end of the interview. Your hand's been shaken, and you're alone on the steps, and if he's watching you from the other side of the glass you can't see him, but you doubt it. You don't look back again until you reach your car. Then you take one last look up at the building, and you know that Gordon Snider is watching from one of those five hundred windows, but you can't see him either. You can't see anybody.

SMALL DEATH

When Wyn's friend Carl came to town to give a talk called "Book Art, Book Design" at a publishers' convention, Wyn kept looking at him and thinking there was something he wanted to tell him, and then he'd remember it was Susan Hilliard and think *Uh-oh*.

In the rec room Wyn's wife Janet had set up an IKEA kid's cot they'd bought in case their daughter's friends wanted to stay over, but Wyn suggested he and Carl carry down the futon from the living room instead. This they started to do, but when Carl, who didn't (as Wyn secretly knew) like futons, realized how heavy it was he said he preferred the cot.

"If the cot's uncomfortable, I can always slip the mattress off and sleep on the floor. It's carpeted down there, right?"

The whole bed-for-Carl thing was a knot in Wyn's mind. Ever since they'd known Carl was coming, Janet had been after Wyn to buy a third futon to keep in the rec room for guests, but Wyn was fed up with futons, which were too heavy to be fluffed, or whatever you were supposed to do to them, and besides, he and Janet were $9,000 into his Personal Line of Credit on top of the mortgage, and he'd said no, partly because of being fed up with futons, partly because of the overdraft, and partly because Janet's consumer solution to the problem failed to address the disparity between the labour necessary to earn enough to pay the new bill and the labour of carrying a futon down and up the stairs a couple of times a year. But he didn't argue any of this, because Janet had heard it before, on other occasions, and it only made her lips go thin. Instead Wyn argued that when he himself stayed at Carl's he was expected to sleep on any old thing, once even on a sheet of that clear plastic with the little bubbles, used for packing. The fact was, Wyn told Janet as they were doing the dishes one night, Carl was the last person on earth to notice what people, including himself, were sleeping on. Or with, he added. Janet, who used to sleep with Carl, flicked Wyn with the dish towel.

In order to satisfy himself the cot would do for Carl, Wyn lay on its flimsy foam mattress and tried to imagine eight hours of this. As he shifted his body, absorbing the strange cheap buoyancy of the thing, he remembered that the last time Carl slept over, before the rec room was finished, he'd put him in the living room on a futon that was too short. The next morning, when Wyn asked him how he'd slept, Carl had answered, Diagonally. Wyn moved around on the cot not believing Carl while Carl told him to stop worrying, the cot would be fine. To make up for the cot, Wyn found Carl an extra-large towel and hauled an enormous quantity of bedding out of the rec room cedar closet. One guest had complained about being cold down here.

Wyn also offered Carl the freedom of the books in his office. As he led the way down the hall from the rec room, he imagined that Carl would want to read in bed, the way he himself liked to do when he stayed over at other people's houses, sampling a pile of their books. Earlier they'd been talking about *Granta*, the magazine, and that same day, while Carl was out, a new issue happened to arrive, so first Wyn showed him that. The title of the issue was *What Went Wrong?* On the cover was a colour close-up of a dazed Romanian woman talking in a press of people. The forefinger of her bloody right hand was held vertically, a little higher than her forehead, as if she were checking the wind. The top of her hair seemed dark and sticky with blood. The picture continued onto the back cover where a younger Lech Walesa sort of guy was revealed to be standing right up next to her, gazing at her with stolid concentration, his face smeared all over with blood.

On the first page of *Granta*, before the table of contents, was a full-page ad for Bruce Chatwin's autobiography, *What Am I Doing Here*, and that must have been why Carl said,

"You read *Difficult Women*, didn't you? David Plante?"

Wyn nodded. It was Carl who'd told him to read *Difficult Women*.

"Well," Carl said, "did you see in *Esquire*, Plante's written a piece on Chatwin? Victoria says he's doing the same thing to Chatwin he did to the women. I'm not so sure."

Victoria was Carl's wife.

"Was Chatwin gay?" Wyn asked. "Were he and Plante—?"

"No, Chatwin was married. But he died from AIDS."

"I thought Chatwin died from some kind of Chinese fungus."

"Right," Carl said. "AIDS. You die of horrible things nobody's died of for a thousand years. Do you know anybody with AIDS?"

Wyn knew a dozen people with AIDS. He nodded.

"It's horrible," Carl said. "Really horrible."

Wyn nodded.

Gazing at the cover, Carl carried the *Granta* down the hall towards the rec room. Still in his office, wanting to give Carl more books, Wyn kept looking around until he noticed one by Garrett Price, a guy they both used to know at university, a guy about whom Carl had once said that you couldn't tell if he was a genius or just had a funny-shaped head. In fact, when a student of Wyn's had offered to lend him the book, Wyn had used Carl's remark about Garrett Price as his own. He'd been doing this a lot lately, he'd noticed. Practically everything he said came straight from somebody else. Culture in action, he supposed. Viewpoints on the move. The dissemination of the unexamined.

Wyn walked down to the rec room and handed Garrett Price's book to Carl. It was a quality paperback called *A Checkered Future*. Looking at it, Carl said,

"Nice cover. I heard the guy who did the artwork has AIDS."

Wyn didn't say anything. He couldn't.

Carl glanced up.

"This seems to have astonished you. I thought that was the connection."

"No," Wyn said. "The connection was Garrett Price."

Carl continued to look at the book.

"Anyway," he said. "I'm sure he's the one."

"I don't think it's very good," Wyn said.

"The cover?"

"The book. Not that I've—" Wyn swallowed.

"Pardon?"

"Not that I've read it."

"OK title. Sort of."

"This is goodnight," Wyn said.

"Yes," said Carl, looking up absently from Garrett Price's book. "Goodnight."

Wyn went upstairs. In the kitchen he set up the coffeemaker and arranged the table for breakfast. He put away the dishes in the washer. When Wyn was afraid, his assumptions slowly took off their disguises and stood before him as injustices the world had only ever tolerated. When Wyn was afraid, the world grew sulky and resentful and loomed as if it would crush him if it could.

Janet was already in bed. She was under the eiderdown with her knees up. She smiled at Wyn and lowered her lids in a way that for a vague reason annoyed him.

"How was Carl's talk?"

Janet whispered because Carl was in the room directly below them.

"Fine," Wyn whispered back. "Carl's smart."

At that moment he couldn't remember what Carl's talk had been about. He changed out of his clothes and into the T-shirt he slept in and went into the bathroom and closed the door.

Garrett Price's publisher's cover designer, Eric McSomebody, the one who seemed to have AIDS, had also done the cover for Susan Hilliard's book, and she'd had an affair with him.

Wyn left the bathroom and got into bed with Janet, who said,

"Anything more about it you want to tell me?"

"It—?"

"The talk. Like, who was there?"

"Publishers."

"No kidding."

Wyn turned out the light and waited for Janet to move onto her left side so he could cup his body to hers until she was warm and he was too warm and had to move away, onto his other side, but instead Janet raised her left knee slightly and took his fingers and put them between her legs. She was very wet. Slowly at first, she moved against his fingers. After a little of this, her hand went to him, but he held it and pressed it against the mattress. Janet moved harder against his fingers. The bed creaked.

"I think I'm going to have to—" Janet whispered.

She sighed.

Her breath was ragged.

When her body quieted she said, "You were worried Carl'd hear."

"Can't say the idea affects me the way it does some people."

"Oh you scumbag." She kissed him. "So who'd you pretend you had your fingers up? In the dark."

"I'm shocked."

206

She kissed him again. "You don't have to tell me."

"You think I'd dare?"

But that wasn't it. Imagination didn't bother Janet, only betrayal.

Four days last month Wyn had spent at a modern literature conference in Kansas City, and with one thing and another the whole trip was sex. Sometimes this happened but not usually so completely. Usually when Wyn travelled on his own, if he wasn't too busy or exhausted, he sank into a state of low-grade arousal, leaden anonymity, pulled by the magnets of adult bookshops or grimly back to his hotel room and the perineal tedium of the adult channel. Strange cities Wyn found harsh. Arousal could foil a pitiless hotel room, and afterwards the difference, the plummet to pitiless, was loony-tune. Maybe animals were sad after sex but not Wyn, who found everything mildly hilarious, for a couple of minutes. The world had changed, it hadn't changed, it had changed for not having changed, it hadn't changed.

Within an hour of entering his Kansas City hotel room Wyn had found in the bedtable drawer a Gideon New Testament with a *Your Comments Please* card for a bookmark. The card, completed by "You're greatful custumer, Dale Platt," in a childish stubby pencil, began "Dear sir, thank you verry much for your kingsize bed." Mr. Platt went on to catalogue his various points of entry into the body of his girlfriend in the appreciated bed, concluding, "In other words she has been having 'a full life' in more ways then one thanking you."

Next to the New Testament was a paperback forgotten by Mr. Platt. Its title, *Violent Tales of Enema Domination*, failed to prepare Wyn for dreamlike pastoral accounts of enemas administered to nubile Heidis by kindly old gentlemen in lederhosen.

Janet had benwah balls on her Christmas list, so after speed-reading *Violent Tales*, Wyn went out into the Kansas streets in search of these items, but the salesman in his Stetson, who'd never heard of benwah balls, regarded Wyn with eyes no less wary of oriental perversion than of Canadian mental illness. Hapless Wyn he steered on a tour of the all-American wares on display here at For Lovers Only, but at inexorable speed and to a sales pitch repetition-weathered to erasure and misinflection. And either because he'd never heard the word or because he thought it was more genteel to shorten the vowel or because this was how they pronounced it in Kansas City, he kept saying "annal."

"Now this one here, Sir. Note the smaller diam'ter, for her annal enjoyment."

Wyn thought he must be saying "animal."

"*Animal*?" he asked finally and was shaken to glimpse under the Stetson eyes of death-force menace.

All so far recountable to Janet back home with drinks on a Friday night, but then at the opening reception Wyn met Susan Hilliard, an actual living woman with a scary intelligence, who laughed and shook her head and reached out with both hands and popped him down the middle like a milkweed pod. "Are we going to do anything?" One moment he and this beauty were facing each other across a certain din, hipshot, wineglasses in hand, foreheads grazing, laughing a lot, and the next, well— Being almost complete strangers (he'd read her book), they'd wasted only a few minutes, and these hung in the turmoil of the air for a sign that when they lifted each other up it had better be all the way up, fathoms up, thirty-two-feet-per-second-per-second up, up through the bloodroot and the crimson pear, up through the creamy cream of the maypop, the spittle and the mustard and the muck and the guts, splayed and yearning, ascending faster and faster with necks stretched and twisting, writhing, up and up, up so far that if they'd gone any higher they'd have bled and sweated away together into that sodden ruined mattress, that Simmons Sleeprite of Mutual Slaughter.

And then she was gone, and Wyn's universe was a picture window with a network of cracking that made its tentative, exploratory way to every edge and corner of the frame, and when it had it all covered, the entire surface, nothing happened, everything held, intricate and full, beautiful in its damage. Until, in sheets and great handfuls, onto the sill, into the shrubbery, onto the broadloom, onto Wyn's shoes, it fell. Heavy as flesh.

Wind and darkness blasting his eyes.

A month later things were pretty well OK, Wyn had a picture window again, and life was not so webbed and entangled by lying. Susan Hilliard was a headful of images repetition-weathered to erasure and misinflection, and Wyn was safe as usual at the end of the day in his own bed in his own house with his own family, except that nothing was OK, nothing. None of this. His mind, which should have been busy with the unfinished bits of the day, all the tiny miscues, instead was sitting up like a smashed animal grooming itself, like a decrepit lawyer adrift in the bedclothes, struggling to recuperate, to flush, to annul, in a hemorrhage of denial, on a thousand technicalities, this fresh, fatal knowledge.

How he'd come within an inch of not going to the conference this year. How the approach to bed with Susan Hilliard was like a pebble taking a certain downhill path: predict each bounce before you call it inevitable. There were too many alternatives to how that sixty-minute mating dance could have gone, too little reason for it to have gone any one of them. The wrong word, a hint of pursuit or presumption, too light or too heavy a tone. How unlikely it was he'd ever hear about this Eric McSomebody. The chain of circumstance was too fragile, it couldn't hold. Why should truth get to grow strong by drinking the blood of its own unlikelihood? A quiet-spoken neighbour lad guns down his parents, and suddenly nobody has any doubt how to read that soft presence. The high beams of the second guess. It's not fair to see so clearly today when yesterday you couldn't see anything at all.

Wyn rolled back onto his left side, and as he moved he noticed how completely healthy he was, how strong and sound. He felt as if he'd just taken five 222s with a big glass of warm milk.

Janet was already asleep. Across the hall, his daughter. Downstairs he heard Carl cough.

At five-thirty a.m. Wyn drove Carl to the airport in the dark, and they talked about publishing. Outside the terminal, in the dark morning, feeling like a little cartoon person reaching up out of a black wash of pain, Wyn shook Carl's hand and wished him a good flight. As he did this, he could feel the love—or was it fear?— flowing down his arm and out through the palm of his hand into Carl's.

Carl was looking at him oddly.

"How'd you sleep?" Wyn wondered, and tears were standing in his eyes.

I love this guy, Wyn thought. And then he thought, *Why be sentimental?* And then: *But I do.*

"Perfectly," Carl replied. "Unlike yourself."

Wyn nodded. He had forgotten what Carl was talking about.

"Plane," Carl said, glancing over at the doors.

Wyn looked down and saw that he was still gripping Carl's hand.

"This is goodbye," Carl said.

From the airport Wyn drove straight to his office and at

twenty past nine her time got through to Susan Hilliard. There was one of those nonrecognition pauses.

Wyn said his name again. Still nothing.

"Kansas City," he said. "Last month."

"Oh. Hi."

It was an airy querying wariness that Wyn happened to know, a dangerous placidity, and he was pretty sure what it said:

No matter how carefully I choose, how high I aim, it comes to this. An apparently nice guy, mature, not stupid, a sense of humour, you climb in, climb out, say goodbye. You wait a few days and here he is on the line, diminished. Too small now to understand that from here on it's just your pain and concerns and expectations and priorities and his pain and concerns and expectations and priorities. And the conclusion is always the same: Either all men are jerks, or I am only attracted to jerks.

"Listen," Wyn said, trying to be firm, though his voice shook. "I'm worried about something, and I wanted to talk to you about it."

"Can I call you back?"

"No. I just heard your friend Eric has AIDS."

"Who told you that?"

Wyn explained, without naming Carl.

"Somebody out there's confused. Eric's happily married."

"Is he."

"Yes he is. I'm his wife's best friend. Angela's great. They're the tightest couple in the world. Your friend's wrong. But you're very sweet to—the thing is, I know Eric very well."

"That's what I mean—"

"Oh, you asshole. Isn't that funny. First I call you sweet and then I call you an asshole. I'm sorry, Wyn. Wyn. What an unusual name. But I really do have to go. It was two years ago. I told you that."

211

"Will you have a blood test?"

"A blood test? Are you serious? I'd kill for Eric."

"That's what I'm worried about."

Susan laughed. "I just meant now that he's so sick, into hospital with pneumonia every few weeks, and of course Angela's hardly out of her coma any more, but all I've got's these bumps all over my body—"

"*Don't!*"

"Did you hear me? Two years. More than two years."

"Would you believe ten."

"You need a lesion, a break in the skin."

"Not necessarily."

"Listen. Forget this. You've got the guilts and I'm on my way to a meeting. You think you've been *so bad* that only the worst kind of death could be punishment enough. Well, it sounds like little-boy stuff to me. Have a blood test yourself."

Susan Hilliard hung up.

Wyn looked at the holes in the earpiece of the receiver. Then he put down the phone and sat at his desk looking out at the parking lot in the grey dawn. She'd be bracing with a whip, that one. Madam Certainty. She knew nobody was going to die from the trivial thing that had been done. She understood that this was no pipe-sucking Freudian death wish, at least not one with fulfillment potential. She knew little-boy stuff when she saw it.

Wyn tried to think clearly. He'd told Susan his friend had named Eric, but Carl hadn't actually said a name, had he, only that it was the guy who did the cover.

Wyn took down Susan Hilliard's book, *The Whole Duty of a Feminist*. On the dustjacket it said, "Cover design by Eric McTeal." McTeal. He then reached for Garrett Price's book, as if he had ever kept it at his office and it was not still on the floor beside Carl's cot in the rec room.

Wyn called home. His daughter answered sleepily.

"Karen, sweetheart, is Mum there?"

"She's sleeping."

Wyn looked at his watch. It wasn't six thirty.

He explained to Karen what he needed. After some searching, she was reading out proudly, "Cover design by Eric McTeal."

"Great! Thanks, sweetheart!"

"It was on the back. Who's he?"

"Nobody. It's just a name for a, list I have to do. It's boring. Anyway, thanks."

"OK. Bye, Dad."

Wyn sat at his desk and cried. Then he cancelled his nine o'clock lecture by going down to the classroom before anybody got there and writing on the blackboard. After that he went to the Red Cross blood clinic at the university hospital. As he lay back on the bed he said to the nurse,

"What if I have AIDS?"

"Then you shouldn't be giving blood."

"But what if I don't know?"

The nurse, a black woman, paused holding the tourniquet to look at him.

"If you don't know, then you don't have AIDS. What you mean is, you don't know if you're HIV positive."

"Right."

"We'll tell you," she said.

"But I thought it could take three or four months to show up."

"Don't worry. We'll tell you."

As the blood drained from his body, Wyn decided that the fact he would call Janet at 6:30 in the morning was a good sign. It meant that he was working to punish himself by alerting his wife. This was just the boy, wanting the world to unfold the way it does when you're four.

Outside the hospital the day was cold and sunny. It shocked Wyn to see how shameless the streets were with their reassurance. Not a dream, a conscious lie. He walked until he came to the river, studded with floes, the whole width of it sliding away. He looked down at the water's edge touching his shoes. He couldn't not make love with Janet for three months. He looked up to the blue vacancy of the sky. But what if it was already too late? He looked at his watch and was amazed to see how early it was. He'd still be in the classroom. If time had forked, he still was. You veer off and you're gone. You visit another city and you leave the main course of your life. But anonymity's hard, death seems everywhere. Sex is a little thing in itself, pathetic, a bit of grit, an itch you pearl with fantasy to change things for a few minutes, to change nothing at all. People leave their identities, and then they sigh and take them up again. They'd be crazy not to. There's less-organized will and then there's more-organized will. There's desire and then there are the proprieties of who we are. It's not the body, the body's a playing field, it's the simpler level of abstraction. A diversion. What's to forgive? The crime would be to say anything. The inappropriate need to suffer.

Oh please let this be just him. Let him go down with the artists and the intellectuals. The world won't stand blithely by.

And dear God, remove me from this fool.

Later that day, from a phone booth, sweating and shaking, Wyn called Carl, over and over. No answer. At last he got him, just in the door from the airport. And as Wyn, breathless with fear, told his friend everything, he knew this was exactly the wrong thing to do, he could feel himself dredging the words from some arbitrary and specious place, but he hoped it might be how he could pay what he owed, and he forced himself to say it all.

When Wyn stopped talking there was a pause, and Carl said,

"McTeal's the designer. It's the guy who did the artwork that McTeal used who's sick. I told you that. Your conscience must really be bothering you."

Immediately Wyn knew he should not have said anything to Carl.

"Now I feel stupid," he said.

"You are stupid," Carl said. "Janet's better than you deserve, and Karen's a wonderful kid."

"I never don't know that," Wyn said.

"So you can be relieved now," Carl said.

"I will, believe me," Wyn said. "And I'm really sorry I bothered you with this."

"Don't think about it."

Three years later, at a conference in New York State, Wyn felt instant sympathy with a woman named Sharon, a Dean at the University of Delaware. It was a break from their lives. Four years after that, Sharon wrote with bad news about a lover she'd had, on and off, for almost twenty years.

At first Wyn wondered why she'd tell him. He thought the fear must have made her sentimental.

Printed in Canada